Originating from England and having travelled throughout Canada, the author currently resides in beautiful British Columbia. Spending part of the year in the Cascade Mountains of Northern Washington, USA, she enjoys walking with her northern canine friend and howling to the moon with the coyotes around the camp fire.

Her life has been dedicated to the rescue of dogs and enjoying the natural environment.

The author's first novel, *Olive*, a historical fiction, was released in August 2017. Her second book, *Full Circle*, is also a historical fiction.

Dedicated to a wanderer who found love along life's path, and peace and solace in a canine friend.

Linden Carroll

FULL CIRCLE

AUSTIN MACAULEY PUBLISHERS™
LONDON • CAMBRIDGE • NEW YORK • SHARJAH

A CIP catalogue record for this title is available from the British Library.

ISBN 9781788781442 (Paperback)
ISBN 9781788783187 (Hardback)
ISBN 9781528955898 (ePub e-book)

www.austinmacauley.com

First Published (2019)
Austin Macauley Publishers Ltd
25 Canada Square
Canary Wharf
London
E14 5LQ

While a fictional piece of work, this historical novel is based in part on facts and extracts from a friend's life shared, albeit with some degree of trepidation.

Prologue

This is a story of the indomitable spirit of a youth into manhood; his earliest years spent growing up in the war-ridden city of London, England.

12 years old and orphaned following WW2, he follows a clandestine lifestyle on the London streets while England rebuilds after the war. His rescue of another teen from the streets and their liaison cause him to experience the pain and intensity of first love and parenthood subsequently separating them.

Becoming a seafaring adventurer, he spends many years travelling across England and Canada finally returning to his homeland to reclaim his lost love and their daughter.

This novel follows the path of an orphaned boy and all consuming, undying love, spanning more than 50 years ebbing past the physical, flowing into every hidden corner of the mind and flooding the very soul to eternity.

Chapter 1
A New Life

Coldness engulfed him, the like of which he had never experienced before, as he stood quietly over her lifeless body. Her face glowed with a calmness unfamiliar to him. Her arms were clasped tightly to her as if she were in prayer; those arms which would never hold him and comfort him again. She was dead, he knew that but for a moment, refused to acknowledge the stark nakedness of truth staring up at him. Reality took him suddenly in its deadly embrace and he knew that he would never ever again be loved in the way she had loved him. Her poor body worn out with overwork, lack of nourishment and day-to-day struggles had fought a valiant war but her weak heart finally ceased to fight any longer. Shuddering, he knelt beside her and prayed, his young voice harsh with emotion.

"Dear God, although you don't seem very dear to me at this moment, you look after this fine lady. She did her best for me and everybody else. She was too good for this rotten world you put her in and left her alone to look after herself. You may have thought you were doing the right thing when you took my dad to be with you but you were wrong, so you make things up to her and do the right thing by her. Give her all the pretty things she always dreamed of, silk dresses and flowers, lots and lots of flowers. I'm looking to you to make it happen."

He stayed for a while, the memory of her image boring into his brain until his head ached, enervating his being, overwhelming him with grief. A sudden rush of adrenalin propelled him to his feet and up the stairs to his little bedroom where he threw his few belongings in a bag. Reaching up to the top shelf in the cupboard, he found the little tin box that held all his documents and an emergency supply of cash. They had both agreed the money was to be used only in the direst of emergencies; this was certainly one and to his relief, there was a sizeable sum. She'd always tried to keep him safe. Seizing upon it gratefully, he rushed downstairs pausing for one last look on his way out. *I'd better get going*, he thought, *they'll be coming for me as soon as this gets out*, so he hit the street running and didn't look back.

Twelve years old, almost thirteen but going on 30, he'd just lost his mother, his only parent and was about to embark on his new life with no home and nobody in this world to care or give a damn or so he thought.

****

Born in 1938 at a time of enormous unrest with the pending war, his mother had named him Alexander after Alexander the Great. She always relayed the story of Alexander the famous warrior.

"Alexander was a great king you know, a genius in all military aspects. He ruled Greece and much further across to Egypt and even India way before Jesus was even born. Everywhere he went he brought all the trades and business together and everybody ended up speaking Greek which became the common language for doing business. Can you believe that? He was the most powerful of kings when he was only in his twenties and ruled for more than ten years but he didn't die in one of his battles, it was a stupid cold that did him in. So you have to make sure you always wrap up warm in the cold weather and take your cod liver oil each morning, that's the best thing to keep the colds away."

Alex would always think of those words as he was choking on the huge yellow cod liver oil capsule each morning. It was only the thought of how strong and invincible he was going to be that kept him from throwing it right back up.

Smiling down at him, she always finished off with, "And that's why you're named after him. He was a king and you are my little king."

Unfortunately, as people always do, his name was shortened and he became known as Alex.

"Yes Alex, you're my king just like your dad was. He was strong and brave, and loved us very much. He went to war to fight the enemy just like Alexander and won the battle so that we could have a better life. He died on the battlefield but he's up in heaven now watching over us."

Alex noted that his mother's eyes always filled with tears at this point and she would hang onto him so tight that it hurt but he never said a word, he just wanted to make her feel better.

"Well I'm the man of the house now and I'm going to look after you just like Dad would have wanted."

She would laugh; he always loved her tinkling laugh, like a lovely clear stream running over the pebbles in some magic place. Bending down, she would kiss him all over his face, *goofy girl's stuff* he thought, tasting the salt in her tears but still he said nothing, just let her hold him close until she started chattering girlie talk again, like go and tidy up his room and put all his toys away, waste of time really because they would just be coming out of their box again.

He had been too young to know what was happening in the early years but as he grew and the war advanced, he got the picture with amazing clarity in spite of his youth. After his dad was killed, he would hear his mother crying herself to sleep at night, mourning over the loss. Sometimes he would tap on her door and pretend he'd just had another nightmare and ask if he could stay with her for a while. Comforting him always made her forget her immediate sadness.

His most vivid memories of the war years were of the struggling to hang onto her as they practically fell down steps to the cellar when they heard the approaching enemy planes. Pre-war houses were built with extra big cellars and this was no exception. His mother always kept basic provisions in the cellar in case they had to remain there for long periods of time and on many occasions neighbours, who got caught in the volley of bombs, joined them if they were too far from their own shelters. Alex's mother never failed to lay herself over him to protect him from the fearful attacks. He remembered always the warmth of her body and the fierce grip of her arms around him. She would always start singing to blot out the noise of war and her beautiful voice rang out through the basement, almost obliterating the sounds of the terrible explosions, not quite but almost until everybody else joined in making such a din they drowned out the noise. Once they even had to shelter in the underground tube station to get away from the bombs but they only did it the once because the gas mains were getting bombed and spreading gas everywhere. They could easily have been choked in the underground tunnels. He shivered at the thought, although they may have had a chance with the gas masks that the government had given everybody to carry around with them in little cardboard boxes. Everybody looked like aliens who had come down to earth from another planet when they were wearing the masks.

Suddenly it was all over, the atrocities of the time expended and the battle won. Everybody seemed happy to Alex and they were singing and dancing in the streets and celebratory parties were rampant everywhere. Flags and banners were hoisted, with rosettes and buttonholes proudly displayed in shop windows, all showing the red, white and blue colours of the British flag.

Even though the fighting had stopped and war was over, everybody still had to be very careful with food, never wasting a thing as it was always in short supply. Alex learned never to ask for seconds because he knew it made his mother sad and she would try to take it off her own plate to give him more.

The food rationing program, which was introduced at the onset of war, was designed to make sure that basic varieties of food groups were available, although the people were still struggling. Different coloured food books had been issued for specific groups of people. Alex remembered the little blue ration books which were especially for children. His mother always told him that the government was making sure little children like him would get enough to eat and she would occasionally give him a carrot on a stick to chew; he always thought that was great fun.

****

One day his mother sat listening to the wireless. Leaping up suddenly, she grabbed her bag and his hand. Stuffing his hat and coat on him, when they reached the hallway she was breathless with excitement.

"Come on Alex. There is a huge victory parade leaving from Regents Park soon. Let's go, come on hurry up."

Both of them were trying to tie his shoe laces at the same time and this was a job that couldn't be hurried; it always took him a painstakingly long time to accomplish.

The pair rushed to see the military parade of the Navy, Airforce, Civilian Services and the Army which had just begun. It was going to end up back at the park but they didn't want to miss any of it. What a sight it was with over 500 vehicles spreading more than four miles down the road. Alex always remembered that day and the excitement of hundreds of spectators.

****

The details of their move back to the city centre escaped the little lad but as time passed, he knew his mother was sick. He tried to help in every way he could but she was getting weaker and forced to place him in care at regular intervals. Those were the worst memories for him. He was quick to catch on that his foster parents were only in it for the money that the government paid them to take in needy kids. Alex had run away many times and was repeatedly hauled back by the authorities. Following the last incident, he had told his mother what happened to him in the foster homes. She clasped her son tightly to her and although aware of how sick she was, vowed he would be staying with her to the bitter end but by God that boy would learn how to survive and be resilient; she would teach him everything she knew.

"Alex you're a big boy now and you know that your mum is not in the best of health. We have to work together and help each other in every way we can and I know I can count on you and don't you worry, you are not being sent away again."

She became very serious then and continued…

"Alex if anything ever happens to me and you are alone; you are to go to Uncle Frank, he'll always help you."

Finally on that fateful day, he had found her on the kitchen floor.

****

Keeping to the alleys and back streets, he made his way through the city which he knew so well without too much incident except for a policemen, helmet askew and billy club flying, hurtling down the street in pursuit of some thief or maybe even a killer. *Who knew and who really cared*, he was thinking, melding his body into an alcove and hunkering down behind a group of dustbins and garbage. He was well versed in disappearing having been always on the run from the abuse dished out to him when he was in foster 'care' and knew the score in spite of his tender age.

****

He thought about the early years when his mother would come to his room to say goodnight and invariably ended up telling him about how wonderful his father had been before the war had come and ruined everything. His dad was taken from him before he ever really had a chance to get to know him and now his mum as well. It wasn't fair. "It's not bloody fair," he ranted, knowing swearing was forbidden but right at that moment, he couldn't give a fig; all he knew was that he was well and truly on his own.

His mind refused to let go of those horrendous years before his dad had died. He could almost smell the fear which swept over his mother every time the postman brought some mail, leaving her trembling and reaching for a chair until she had opened whatever was delivered. Only then did she smile at him saying that there was nothing to worry about. He was lucky though, at least he got to spend some time with his mother. She would not have him evacuated to the country as his friends had been, she was so afraid of him being alone with strangers, particularly if anything should happen to her, what would become of her son? His mum was determined to keep him with her until the bitter end. Alex did wonder from time to time what had become of his friends after their mothers had sent them away.

So mother and son stayed together for the duration and even though he was just a child, the sounds of war were imbedded in his brain. The howling and wailing of the air raid sirens, followed by the drone of hundreds of planes, and that deadly whine and boom of the dreaded doodle bugs, the flying bombs which he associated with death and destruction. He had never seen so many people crying as they tramped through the wreckage searching for missing family members. Broken glass was everywhere when the windows had been blown out with the force of the explosions. He had trouble lifting his legs there was oh so much glass. Then there were the huge silver whales floating up in the sky, barrage balloons his mother had told him, filled with gas and sent up to scare off the enemy; he'd been in awe the first time he saw those.

****

He must have fallen into a deep sleep because suddenly he was awakened by shrieks of one of thousands of feral cats which had just caught something; maybe a mouse or better still a rat. It was fairly close because he could hear its maniacal gurgles of joy as it devoured its meal. *Oh well, everything has to survive I suppose*, he thought, *I might even get to that before I'm through.*

Readying up his belongings, he made his way up the alley towards a tap behind one of the shops where he would freshen up. Dusk was beginning to fall; if he got a move on he would be able to make it to the old bakery shop. Old Frank had always been good to him in the past and would give him any left-overs after the day's business. All the local merchants knew him and had always backed him up in the bad times but it wouldn't be long before word was out and the authorities would be looking for him. Unsure of whom he could trust, he knew he would have to leave the immediate area soon. Where would he go after he had seen Frank?

Suddenly he remembered Bob, a family friend, who lived in Camden Town. Bob had relatives and contacts all over the city and was really in the know. He had a little pawnshop and had a bit of a locksmith business going. He'd heard talk that Bob's business involved some shady stuff, just hearsay but Alex always assumed that he earned a bit on the side with a little safe cracking orthodox and unorthodox. Being situated in north London, in Camden Town, Bob was far enough away from the immediate area which would suit Alex just fine.

Camden Town was vaguely familiar to Alex from the time he and his mother had lived there during the war. They had spent time in Chalk Farm, Regents Park and Primrose Hill. Yes that's what he would do; he would head for Camden Town and call on Bob. With a bit of luck he would be able to do some odd jobs for him and might learn a bit about the trade, locks and security systems had always fascinated him. His spirits lifted. Renewed strength and vigour surged through his veins.

"Yes," he shouted, "I'm resilient, that's what I am. Me mam always said that."

Chapter 2
London's War

Alex's father, James, had been a docker in the Southampton Docks and fortunately his work had been fairly steady. He felt proud of the fact that he had played a part, albeit small, in the development of that area, particularly the Western Docks where construction had begun in the late 1920s and ran until the early 1930s, allowing for much larger vessels to be accommodated.

Upon completion of the docks, James participated in the dismantling of all the fixtures from the Mauretania, a massive passenger ship which had been constructed in the early 1900s. The vessel was being taken out of service by 'The Cunard Line' as it was superseded by the 'Queens' and considered obsolete. Following a varied career, the Mauretania was initially a passenger ship, then a hospital and troopship during WW1 and was subsequently refitted at Southampton to resume service as a passenger ship in its later years. A huge auction was held in the docks of all the ship's fixtures and fittings prior to the vessel heading north for disassembling in 1935.

James had met Grace, his future bride, just by chance when they collided in the High Street and her groceries were strewn half way down the street. Rushing to salvage what they could and colliding once again, they collapsed on the pavement helpless with laughter. The following weeks found them madly in love and typical of lovers with no rationality they married at the first opportunity.

When their baby boy was born they were completely besotted. One night James suggested they move to Primrose Hill in London where his aging mother was living.

"Grace dear, you have no family or relatives and mum can really help out with the little lad. It would really take the load off my mind if you're agreeable."

The suggestion made sense, so they uprooted and moved to London.

****

James' mother had a ground floor suite in one of the large Victorian houses nestled amongst the many bordering Primrose Hill. Beautiful homes with detailed lace curtain panels hanging in the bay windows surrounded by embossed brickwork and elaborate mouldings. Unfortunately, her mother-in-law's house had fallen into disrepair but the living space seemed huge compared to their recent accommodation, with three bedrooms and plenty of room to accommodate all of them. Grace found the kitchen almost intolerable, however, nothing much but an alcove with a curtain across to block it from the rest of the living space. The lack of space in the alcove was coupled with the lack of gas. She had noticed that they were getting less and less gas for their money, because typical of those times, the greedy landlord adjusted the meter practically every time he came, forcing Grace and her mother-in-law to put more and more shillings in the slot. Once the shilling's worth of gas had been used, it would automatically shut off. Cooking a meal was becoming more and more expensive, and cold food became the norm to conserve energy.

The house had been the family home but as her mother-in-law had been widowed when she lost her husband in WW1 and left with children, she had no option but to sell. The buyer immediately divided the house up into flats and crammed as many people in as he could. James' mother was very accepting of the situation, although it must have been heartbreaking to see the change in her old home but she was getting on in years and didn't want to move from the area. A lovely patio garden, not huge but very beautiful with a paved courtyard and a big wrought iron gate bordering the front of the property, had been kept up reasonably well. The back garden, however, was completely overgrown, unused for many years and left to go wild, evidenced by the gorgeous perfumed dog rose which threatened to overcome every other plant in the garden, being extremely invasive by nature. It was interesting to note that because citrus fruits were unavailable during these pre-war times, the government was encouraging people to gather rose hips wherever possible for the vitamin C, which their diet sorely lacked. Even back in ancient times, rosehips had been recognised for their medicinal qualities. In fact Grace had read that the great Roman Naturalist Pliny (AD 23) upheld the belief that the dog rose was named such because the root cured the bite of a mad dog.

The long narrow lot was surrounded by a huge red brick wall, common in Victorian houses. Grace would sometimes venture onto the perimeter fascinated by the abundance of life. Because of the garden's unkempt state it was home for many little creatures, weaving their way in and around the tangled undergrowth and undisturbed wilderness. A massive blackberry bush trailed down the wall with the biggest, sweetest blackberries Grace had ever seen or tasted for that matter. She would gather them into a bowl and make pies, cramming as many into the oven as would fit to conserve power. No self-respecting Brit would turn the oven on unless every available bit of space was put to use.

One night at dinner, Grace broached the subject she had been pondering all day. She had not wanted to belittle James in any way but he still hadn't found permanent work and it was getting impossible to manage.

"James, I've been offered a very good steady position in service with a really well-to-do family and I want to take the job. It makes sense, at least until you get fixed up."

Finally, after hashing it out, they both decided that it was indeed for the best and Grace rattled on while she had the advantage.

"And the great thing is that Miranda, that's the lady of the house, said I could take little Alex with me. They have a lovely nursery and it couldn't have worked out better for us at this time. Your mum isn't up to looking after the baby for any length of time; she needs to rest as she's very frail."

Knowing Grace was right, James gratefully acquiesced.

Miranda treated Grace very well and even offered her more work as a nanny in between her domestic chores. Miranda loved little Alex as did the family children and it was a very workable arrangement all round. Grace managed to make ends meet with difficulty as she had never been physically strong. A weak heart aggravated the situation causing her to suffer extreme exhaustion. Miranda was kind and knowing Grace's medical condition went easy on her and made allowances for her bouts of ill health.

****

It was September 3, 1939. Grace was taking the opportunity to relax for a few moments before starting lunch. Her mother-in-law was dozing in the old rocking chair. She had been worried about the old lady who was not herself and seemed to have given up of late. Her gnarled arthritic fingers picked through her food like a small bird foraging for fragments and she spent an inordinate amount of time sleeping, as did her little grandson, who was again sleeping soundly in his crib without a care in the world, while his father was out looking for work.

With the growing unrest and threat of war, James didn't have to look for employment long because he was conscripted by the government. Initially, young men of 20 and 21 years were required to take six months' military training and the RAF had taken over part of Primrose Hill for training purposes. Gradually other age groups were included in the conscription program and soon well over one million joined the forces, the majority going into the Army.

All the uncertainties of life passed through Grace's mind, not the least the recent conversation with her boss. One day, Miranda had sat Grace down in the kitchen.

"I'm sorry Grace but I'm closing up the house. The war is getting much too close to home and I am taking the kids to the country. I'll not be back with them until after this is all over."

Miranda's voice droned on but Grace barely heard. She was stunned and had been relying on the money. Her mind desperately sought a solution.

"Yes, I'll be staying with my sister until this has all blown over. How will you manage, do you think you'll be alright?"

How empty the words seemed to Grace. Miranda had already made her plans and was leaving. Why was she bothering to placate her at this point in the game?

****

Grace sat up abruptly when suddenly broadcasting was interrupted to bring the announcement of the onset of war. Neville Chamberlain, the British Prime Minister, announced that a state of war existed between Britain and Germany.

The enemy started bombing steadily at first; nobody could have imagined what was to come. Nevertheless, in anticipation of the worst, the evacuation of London began and continued for the next few days. Hundreds of cars poured out of the city crammed with families, pets and belongings, in fact anything that could be jammed into the vehicles. They were fleeing to the country. The railway cancelled their plans for their pending strike and herded hundreds of little cockney children into the carriages. They were being evacuated to the country where it was considered they would be safe. Their mothers, bewildered, watched their departure, completely lost without their offspring, wondering when and if they would see them again.

British troops got ready for the onslaught, and mingled with the crowd singing all the old songs, some of which had actually been sung in the First World War. Their enthusiastic patriotism and hilarity spurred everybody on to join with them in the gaiety. All banded together with hearts filled with hope and no idea of what was about to hit them.

Increasing to massive proportions, enemy aircraft filled the heavens and disgorged their bombs unmercifully for more than two months with catastrophic ramifications, changing the face of London forever.

Previous merriment was very soon forgotten. Londoners who did not evacuate now stayed in their homes. Not only did the Blitz bring the city to its knees but also major cities such as Southampton, Liverpool, Manchester and others. One third of London was wiped out superseding that of the Great Fire of London 300 years previously. If the enemy had not been deployed back to Russia, the horror would have continued. The British public enraged at the carnage vowed that what had been started by the German dictator would be continued relentlessly until every vestige of Nazism was overcome and wiped off the face of the earth.

During the Blitz, huge numbers of people forced their way into the underground station seeking protection from the 'reign of terror', which caused the government to reconsider its view that it was not economically viable during wartime to develop the underground as deep shelters running under existing train lines. Several sites were proposed and agreed upon for fitting out as shelters. These were developed in a timely fashion and proved to be of triple value; as a protection for thousands against the onslaught of bombs and following the war, as housing for the Caribbean immigrants and later forming the basis for the new high speed underground tube line development.

****

James was to be shipped out overseas in the morning. The young couple held each other as if their very lives depended on it. They talked and they loved, then they talked again. Fear was in their eyes and echoed in James' words.

"Tomorrow we'll leave our homes and everything that is precious to us. We'll travel paths strewn with monstrous happenings, wishing our feet could follow another course. We won't take life, living, loving, or in fact anything for granted ever again because we'll evolve into different beings and those we love and cherish will also evolve because of the shear fear or reality of losing their loved ones. Oh but it were for a better cause than war, but out of this spiritual metamorphosis will come resilience. Those of us that survive will be strong and those that survive and don't evolve will weaken and die; but you my love are strong, you will survive and evolve to love and nurture our son through the years, possibly without his father by your side. So be brave my dear, we are as untried children in the face of such adversity, only our strength will see us through."

****

War had been raging for four torturous years, the suffering and hardship incalculable both to those valiant souls on the front and those at home bearing the loss of their loved ones. And such was the state of poor Grace.

The telegram lay on the floor and she sat, drained of all energy. Her young husband was dead just as the allies were winning the battle and there was a glimmer of hope that the war would be ending soon. She was never to recover from her grief and neither did her mother-in-law who passed away shortly after.

Grace received a very small widow's allowance from the Army as the wife of a non-commissioned officer. As was the case for many service women, the money was not enough to provide for them adequately, particularly if they had small children. Grace had managed to hang on for as long as she could but with a burden of too high rent decided to move closer into town which, although under heavy siege, offered her a better chance of earning something to supplement her pension. She would give it a shot she decided and if it didn't work out she would take Alex back down south where she had been born. In the interim, she would get in touch with Frank, an old family friend, who owned a bakery closer to the city centre. He would look out for both of them and see them right. Having made a decision, she felt moderately better about her situation. Her Army pension would help until she was able to get some sort of work.

****

The death of the Nazi dictator by his own hand brought about an end to the war. British casualties, while not as high as WW1, were still astronomical. The nation went berserk with joy, singing and dancing in the streets celebrating the end of the wanton killing. Their misery had been exacerbated by years of shortages and food rationing, which unbeknownst to the citizens was to continue on until 1954. Basic necessities such as no hot water and other needs were just a fact of life for many.

Winston Churchill gave his great victory speech and the Royals mingled with the crowds and made appearances on the balcony at Buckingham Palace. The drinkers got drunk and the more pious prayed and gave thanks to their God in the few churches that remained, the majority of those re-built after the great fire of London had been annihilated yet again in this war but the faith lived on.

There were many who were never able to get their lives together again; sorrow over the loss of their loved ones was all encompassing, sapping them of all purpose and motivation rendering them incapable of avoiding the black pit of despair. These poor wretches neither gave thanks nor succumbed to drink.

****

It was 1946 when Grace moved to Clapham with her seven year old son.

Shortly after the end of the war, emphasis was placed on re-building London and housing thousands of displaced and homeless people. The first council high-rise came into being. Grace put her name down for one of the flats but many citizens were in the same boat and as she needed work, she was forced to take accommodation above a second-hand shop which, although adequate, was in an area which left a lot to be desired but it came with the added benefit that she was hired on a part-time basis to work in the shop. The pay was menial but it meant that she could spend time with Alex.

One day Grace saw a small ad in the little café down the road for a part-time waitress. The owner liked her and thought she would be good for trade so he hired her for the early evening shift. Grace was overjoyed, she now had two part-time jobs which worked for her and Alex, and things started to pick up for them. She knew she was not in good shape growing weaker daily but with the new National Health Service which had been brought about following the general election in 1945, she was able to get assistance. Grace, however, was losing the fight, her breathing becoming laboured with even the slightest exertion.

Remembering the last words of her sweet husband, she taught her son resilience and the basic necessities he should always keep to hand. She taught him how to survive on little when there was little of anything, how to sew when the clothes were falling off his back, how to cook and eat when there was little in the pantry and most of all, she taught him to put bitterness aside when life was taking everything he loved and to believe in magic. This she would always emphasise.

"Because magic is all around us," she would say. "We may have to dig for it but it's there just the same, and magic blots out all the bad things that can happen to us, and son," accentuating every word, "If you find you're ever on your own, you go to Uncle Frank."

Whenever she said that, Alex started to get worried.

"But mum you're here, we're together, we're strong and we can handle things."

"Now listen to me. I'm dead serious. If you ever find yourself in trouble or alone, just go to Uncle Frank. Do you hear me?"

He could see she always got agitated at this point trying to catch her breath and dropped the subject hastily.

"Now mum," he would say, "What about a nice cup of tea?"

That always did it and brought everything back to where it was supposed to be.

****

He was a good lad and had befriended a young Jamaican boy they had met when they visited Clapham Common, always a favourite outing for them. The boy had suffered from the racial discrimination which had started to rear its ugly head in Britain. Alex had stood by the young immigrant Daniel, known as Dan, always getting into scraps defending him from the racial bullying, invariably causing him to come home with bleeding knuckles. Even though both were only eleven years old, the boys were to become lifelong friends, almost inseparable. Dan's family was one of the first few hundred immigrants to land on British shores, arriving on 'The Empire Windrush' in 1949. His family and some of their countrymen were temporarily housed in Clapham's deep shelter which had been built to accommodate thousands. These people had been housed by the government in the shelter when it was completed and later dispersed to wherever their labour was needed.

During the development of the shelter, the removal of huge volumes of excavated soils had been a major feat, most of it ending up in Clapham Common increasing the level of the ground and changing the nature of the landscape forever.

Dan's father had been hired by London Transport, as had a large number of the newcomers, with the resultant birth of anarchy in Britain regarding immigration policies and the political agenda; a time of huge unrest. Since the *British Nationality Act 1948* came into effect, at the beginning of 1949, it allowed anyone connected with the UK or one of her crown colonies to become a citizen of UK and colonies, resulting in more troubled times. Dan's family was one of the luckier ones.

****

Grace was filled with relief and gratitude that her son was so independent. Even though he was making his own friends, he was always so attentive to her needs and seemed much older than his years and thank God, so resilient. His dad would have been so proud of him. The two boys would come bursting into the kitchen after another visit to Frank's laden with baked goodies.

Whenever they made a trip to Frank's, they invariably visited an old disused theatre close by. They would stop off and explore the intriguing place all boarded up but like little mice, they had found their way in. The original stage props remained and some old costumes were still intact. The building held unending fascination for the boys and they never got tired of visiting. Little did Alex know that the old theatre was to become a shelter for him in the years that followed.

"Have you been at Frank's Bakery again? I hope you're not making a nuisance of yourselves," Grace would say, always offering up a silent prayer of thanks to God and Frank, when the pair came rushing through the door and arms wrapped around their precious offerings.

Sometimes the boys would travel to Brixton where Dan's family had been relocated, along with many of their countrymen. Alex was always welcomed into the family bosom. Their home, although lowly, was clean and bright, filled with love and caring, and the sounds of Caribbean music. Dan's mother was a huge woman always wearing a voluminous pinafore covered in red tropical-flower prints. How they laughed when she threw up her hands cooing in joy when the boys brought in some of Frank's famous cakes and biscuits. Good old Frank, he always rose to the occasion with his generosity, invariably throwing extra into the bag knowing that the family was sorely lacking in treats of any kind.

One treat however, was forthcoming. Dan's family were all going to the Festival of Britain for the day and asked Alex if he'd like to go with them and of course he jumped at the opportunity.

Set up on the South Bank in 1951, the Festival instilled new public interest and in fact was instigated to boost morale and healing following the devastation of WW2. It featured proposed plans and designs for the rebuilding of London and urban areas. A huge theatre including 3D films, allowing seating for several hundred people, was the biggest attraction but Alex and Dan were in awe at the science centre which boasted the tallest dome in the world. The sea, Polar Regions, space and many futuristic scenes were on show and both boys were bug eyed.

Later, sitting eating fish and chips by the river, the air was filled with their sheer exuberance and exhilarating chatter. What a truly fabulous outing, one that Alex was unlikely to forget, a sentiment which he repeatedly expressed to the good hearted family.

"Thank you for including me in this trip, it was really good of all of you. This has been a day I'll always remember."

Alex was to draw on these good times through all the bad that were to come.

****

"Mum; mum are you there?" Dashing around, he located his mother at the back in the kitchen. She looked up from the newspaper she was reading and Alex couldn't help but notice again how pale she looked.

"Did you have a nice day, Alex?"

"Oh mum it was so great. What a terrific festival, you should have seen the Science Centre."

Smiling enthusiastically, she offered him some tea but he was too excited to have anything, just wanted to recall everything about the day, so she listened, nodding and enjoying the diversion. How happy he was. Her son's face positively glowed with radiance.

Alex slept soundly that night and was up bright and early the next morning. Rushing downstairs to the kitchen still full of enthusiasm from yesterday's events, he came upon his mum lying on the kitchen floor and his life took an abrupt turn, changing him forever.

Chapter 3
Camden Town

Full of resolve, Alex quickened his step. "I must be resilient," he said to himself. "Me mam knew this was going to happen and I have to remember everything she taught me." He knew Frank would still be around, probably in the back alley behind the shop, clearing the debris. His stomach was growling furiously and his mouth watering at the thought of all that good bread and scones, and oh the fruit cake, he really hoped there would be a bit of that left. Frank had been part of his background for as long as he could remember; it seemed he'd known him forever. The old man had always been very good to him and his mother, making a point of saving plenty of left overs for them; kept them under his wing so to speak.

He approached the bakery from the back alley and immediately caught sight of Frank tidying up the garbage at the back after a hard day's work. He looked up when he heard Alex.

"Well hello lad, nice to see you and you picked a good time to come; I've lots of goodies left over. You look as if you've been through a war, what's up lad?"

Concern written all over his face, he dropped what he was doing and led the boy in.

"Let's get some grub down you, never mind leftovers at the moment." Once they were seated, the boy acted as if he hadn't seen food in days and attacked his plate with vigour. Sitting back, hunger finally sated, he looked at

Frank who was very obviously wondering what was going on.

"And how's your mum then?"

For the first time since he had found his mother, Alex broke down, his features contorted in misery. Relaying all that had transpired; he made a point of keeping his eyes downcast so that he wouldn't see Frank's horrified expression lest it weaken him even more, only girls cried after all.

"So here I am. I'm not waiting around here for them to come and get me. Me mam had friends in the Primrose Hill area. The first one I'm going to contact is Bob, he owns a second-hand pawnshop in Camden Town and it's far enough away from here that they won't be looking for me in that neck of the woods."

Frank agreed with him wholeheartedly and shuddered when he thought of the number of boys, particularly orphans who had gone missing from the major homes and orphanages. Nefarious programs were administered by prominent organisations who betrayed the trust of British youth under their care, the aim being to migrate children to the British Colonies for the purpose of colonisation and placement of the boys into trades. Such schemes were initiated in the 1800s to export pauper children because of a perception that placement of such boys into working trades in their homeland was not economically viable. The practice of exporting youth still continued but the focus was on boys older than Alex; nevertheless the risk for him was still high.

Ironic that thousands of British youth, a valuable source of manpower, were banished from their homeland and shortly after the war ended, the first boat carrying hundreds of Jamaicans arrived to escape unemployment in their country and enjoy a better life in Britain; a fact which had been seized upon as an opportunity to re-build Britain after the devastation and destruction reeked upon the country.

Frank resolved to do all he could to get the lad out of the town centre. He had a few contacts that he knew would give the boy a helping hand on his way out of the city. He would have applied to be the boy's guardian but timing was of the essence given the current climate and he would not take the risk, being well aware of many children getting 'lost' in the paper shuffle, particularly orphans.

"Listen Alex, you can lie low with me for the next few days until the heat dies down. I'll get in touch with a few people who will help should you need them on your way out of the city centre. You can sleep on the couch at the back but you'll not be able to leave the place, you hear me? It's for your own good. If they spot you, you're done for and you know that. You and your mam were well known, as sure as shooting somebody will open their face and then you've had it."

"I don't know how to thank you but I don't have nothing to give you."

The boy was grateful and distraught at the same time.

"Enough of that, we don't want to hear talk like that." The other's voice was brusque with emotion. "It's the least I can do, your mum was the best and got the rough end of the deal; never really had a chance but she loved you boy, you were the icing on the cake as far as she was concerned. Talking of cake, you fancy some of that fruit cake you're always on about?"

Alex's mood was elevated and in spite of the abysmal circumstances, smiled across the table at his friend. That night he fell into a deep sleep and for once wasn't pursued by the many demons that came out to haunt him as soon as he drifted into unconsciousness.

The next few days were very satisfying for Alex. Frank was ecstatic; the boy worked unceasingly and was obviously in his element clearing all the irksome jobs that Frank had not been able to get around to do. He was pleased to see that the lad was always careful not to get in sight of the windows in case anybody saw him, staying in the back regions and doing exactly as he was told.

A few days later having arranged some contacts, he called Alex from upstairs.

"Don't know if you remember from your days in Camden Town but there were two stations with conflicting names. One of them is very ancient, it was originally opened in the 1800s called Camden Town but they have just changed the name to Camden Road because there's already the underground (tube) called Camden Town. Alex, I'll make sure my mate puts you on the right line to Camden Town. He'll be here tomorrow to go with you to the station. Here's a map to Sid's bakery, here's how you get there. I've sent word to him that you'll be coming and I've told him he's to take care of you. He's trustworthy Alex, we've been friends a long time and you'll love his wife Elsie as well, she's a real gem, heart of gold."

Alex glanced at the map and could see to his joy that Bob's pawnshop wasn't too far away.

****

The journey to Camden Town went without a hitch and Alex was greeted warmly by Bob and his Mastiff-cross Bruno. Bob had rescued Bruno from certain death when he had stumbled upon the animal cold and half-starved in the alley one winter night. Bob was with a couple of mates and was frantically trying to cover his latest acquisition, a safe of quite large proportions. One of the men had a trolley on which they were easing the safe back into position where it had become dislodged in their haste to get out of the building.

"Crikey what the devil is that?" Charlie had called out looking down at Bob's feet. Their eyes fell on the poor wretched creature. Bob, who had always harboured a soft spot for animals (in fact any helpless creature) reached out and held the dog's face in his hands. Both gazed into each other's eyes and Bob's heart clenched. That was the beginning of a bonding which lasted a lifetime.

Getting the dog home was a bit of a trial but they finally made it, cleaned him up and gave him a juicy steak which was inhaled in seconds it seemed and judging by the speed it went down, it was obvious that he was going to be an expensive addition to the family. Bob named his new companion Bruno, as guessing by the size of his feet, he still had quite a bit of growing to do and appeared to be only about eight months old. Well that was an understatement; the dog never seemed to stop growing and certainly lived up to his name developing into enormous proportions. Bob soon came to realise that Bruno was very obviously descended from the great Old English Mastiff which dated back several thousands of years BC. They generally weighed over 200 lbs. For a while he couldn't stop scrutinising poor old Bruno each day to see whether he had grown since the day before. His canine friend was getting increasing more uncomfortable being the object of his master's intense stare.

The breed had been used in a variety of cruel sports dreamed up by the human species for their amusement and had been almost wiped out. Poor Bruno, however, must have been an outcast and victim of WW2. The lack of food everywhere and costs involved in keeping this type of dog caused many to be abandoned and left to fend for themselves during this period. Bob considered himself very fortunate to have such an amazingly huge but gentle dog. He had noticed that, true to his breed, Bruno was very protective if he felt his owner or their property were threatened in any way and Bob had to make sure he had him under control at all times. A dog of that size could certainly do a lot of damage and Bob was certainly mindful of that. They were devoted to each other and Bob didn't even mind when he was covered in drool every time the great creature laid his head in his lap. As time went by, the two were inseparable.

****

Bruno rushed to Alex and caught him unawares, both crumbling in a heap. The boy laughed uproariously as the massive opponent jumped all over him. Just like old times, they wrestled and rolled around the ground for a few minutes, the dog getting the better of Alex every time just as he had always done. Bob gave Alex a brief hug when he was back on his feet, noting he seemed to have gained at least another inch since the last time he saw him. Not wanting to embarrass the boy, he released him and urged him into the back of the store grinning broadly.

"Well lad, what you been up to, haven't seen you for quite some time? Come into the kitchen, I'll make you some nosh."

They were soon tucking into something delectable that Bob had been stewing up on the stove and there was a huge hunk of bread on a platter along with a generous portion of butter. Alex couldn't get over how well his mother's friends seemed to be surviving the recession following the war. Food rationing was still in effect but they seemed to have plenty to eat.

Alex didn't want to involve Bob in the gory details of his flight out of the city at this time. He felt he should keep a low profile with as little emphasis as possible. He knew Bob didn't follow the news and Alex thought his secret would be safe for some time to come. There was the fact that Bob didn't care much for authority and would be very unlikely to inform them of his whereabouts, nevertheless, Alex did not want to put his friend in a difficult position. The less he knew the better, so he decided to keep quiet and instead embellished on an elaborate yarn that he had been working on since he left the city.

"Mum always wanted to get further out of the city, maybe where she had such happy memories around the Primrose Hill area, so she's taken up night waitressing in one of the bars where she can earn more money. She reckons we should be able to move back this way when she's got a bit of a stake saved so that we can rent something and be together. Rents are cheaper out this way and in the meantime as she can't be with me at night and has to sleep during the day, we decided I'd come and stay with a friend who lives in the area."

The tale just rolled off his tongue, it was so good he almost believed it himself. If only it were the truth. Oh how he missed his mother. 'Resilience son, resilience.' The words bounced around his brain.

"She had always talked about going back south again where she had been born but that's something she said we would decide together at a later date."

Bob seemed to swallow the story.

"You'll be looking to earn a bit of cash yourself then, won't you, so that you can be together sooner?"

“Yes, that’s exactly right. I thought I’d like to come and see you, and ask you if you could teach me the trade. You know I’m right handy with locks and a good many other things.”

Bob smiled fondly at the boy.

“You got that right,” he chortled. “If you was my boy, I’d swear you was a chip off the old block. It’s a real art, that’s what it is and you always had a knack for it even as a little nipper. Don’t think there’s any likelihood of you getting held prisoner for long by anybody.”

Alex, while grinning broadly, quavered inside remembering the number of rooms he had broken out of and ran from abusive foster parents who locked him up for hours, even days without any proper food. No, for sure he wasn’t going to get caught, not ever again.

“When do you think you might have something for me?” he enquired eagerly.

“Well it just so happens that me and the boys is helping a lady out with her safe. We’ll be picking it up from her place and I’ll contact you when we have it. Tell you what, there’s a newspaper seller who ain’t got no legs, they was shot off in the war, when the sods dropped a bomb on the Paternoster Row, he’ll be your contact. Fred always was, and in fact still is, a keen reader. He was high up in the academic field you know, spent hours studying this, that and the other. Anyway, he was having a kip exhausted after his latest research study and paused to rest on the steps just outside the bookshop.

Fred always had his nose in a book and Paternoster Row was the heart of the publishing trade. Do you know it was started in the early 1900s and progressed to the war? Anyway, after that night at the end of December in 1940 more than four and half million books were destroyed, lost forever. The bombing destroyed the whole street. Woke poor old Fred up alright, finds there's nothing much left where his legs was. Lucky to find himself alive, God knows how he made it. Somebody got help and they got him to the infirmary. He's a tough old geezer alright. You'll know him when you see him, he'll be sitting on a little square trolley on wheels; gets himself around on his hands."

Alex had seen dozens of people in London like that after the war. As a little boy, the first time he had seen one such person, he thought the man had his legs locked under him for a joke.

"Hey Mister, that's clever," he had said. "How do you do that, would you show me?"

His mother was chagrined and had left him with no doubt as to the seriousness of his remarks. He was so mortified when he understood that the poor unfortunate had no legs, that the shame of his stupidity stayed with him, making him cringe whenever he looked back on it in later years. It was a miracle these people were still alive, making a living begging or selling leaflets, newspapers, anything they could make a few pence here and there, generally around the stations. The worst were the ones with half their faces shot away. Alex reckoned he would always have nightmares about those.

Bob was still rambling on.

"Yes, you stop by old Fred regularly and he'll give you the details as soon as I pass them to him. Give it a couple of days and then make sure you see him. Now you look done in, do you want to kip here the night? You can get a fresh start in the morning."

Alex was overjoyed, couldn't believe his luck and the hospitality afforded him.

Fully sated after their meal, Bob and Alex relaxed. Suddenly, the room was filled with stench. Bob glared at Bruno who immediately heaved his great hulk up and making a quick snatch for his bone, exited at a fair clip, leaving both Alex and Bob simultaneously diving to open the window. Their riotous guffaws almost raised the roof.

"Sorry about that mate," Bob said a while later, "Mastiffs are prone to flatulence."

"And he sleeps by your bed you tell me; wouldn't want to wake up to that each morning."

Their chortling continued intermittently through their biscuits and tea, and for quite some time after. Needless to say, the culprit remained where he was until he was invited back.

****

Alex readied his possessions up for his trip the next morning and sitting on the edge of the sofa, paused to reflect and make plans.

He would make his base around the Primrose Hill area; commuting from there to Camden Town would be easy with only one stop at Chalk Farm. He had good associations with the whole area and remembered the first time he had heard the Salvation Army Brass Band in Chalk Farm where it was based and had been since it started in the 1880s. He knew that because he had talked to one of the Army Captains that day when he stood with his mum listening. What a great day that had been.

There was an old tree on the outskirts of the park which Alex had come to know well during his excursions with his mother. It had been a hard tree to climb but he had succeeded every time he visited. He was sure it would still be there. About a quarter of the way up, there was a sizeable hole which he'd discovered by chance when a really large woodpecker had surprised him one day. Yes, that would be the perfect place to hide his documents and cash as he built it up and build it up, he would. Later, he would go down to the local bank and open an account. He would never be without again and true to himself, he never was, always having fallback money throughout his life. *Now that's settled*, he thought, *where will I sleep? I know I'll try the old bombed building near the park, hope it's still there*, he mused. He had played around there when he was small and had known it well.

That night Alex went to sleep much calmer, with a much better sense of purpose. Well after all, he had the chance of work, somewhere to sleep and somewhere safe to store his precious belongings.

"Yep, things are sure looking up and I'm hardly underway yet," he said to himself as he settled himself down.

Chapter 4
Primrose Hill

A bright sunny day hailed the next morning. Bob was very hospitable, sparing no effort in ensuring that Alex had every comfort and sat him down to a 'hungry-man' breakfast.

"Get stuck in lad, there's more if you want it."

Alex marvelled yet again at the size and variety of the breakfast. Just like Frank, Bob seemed to be doing alright when most people were not. He wondered how they were doing it. Even Bruno had lucked out, it seemed and was under the table chomping away at an enormous bone with plenty of meat on it; his owner too was eating his way through the biggest portion of bacon that Alex had ever seen.

"So what you doing today lad, got any plans?"

"Well I thought I would get myself settled in. The knapsack is a bit heavy to cart all over the place and I'll look up some people I know."

Alex was thinking of the bakery shop that Frank had put him onto. He was looking forward to meeting Sid and his wife. He knew that Frank would be as good as his word and they would be expecting him and as he was not sure what Frank would have told Sid about him, he had to make sure he was prepared. Eye on the ball as always, Alex was going to make this contact his first port of call as soon as he got settled. He knew he was going to need a leg up here and there, and a bakery could give him practically all his food needs.

After breakfast, he gave Bruno a pat. The dog was much more receptive now that he had cleaned all the meat off his bone and it was safely stashed in his private pantry, a little patch of earth behind the shop, where he could get at it when the fancy next took him.

Bob had given Alex a scrumptious lunch which he stowed away carefully into his knapsack and straightening up, held out his hand formally to his friend.

"Thanks very much for breakfast and everything. I know I'll be able to make myself really useful to you, you'll not regret letting me help out from time to time."

"That I know for sure, you always was a clever hard working lad. I can see you spending a lot of time in the shop too."

Breaking the handshake, he put his arms around the boy and gave him a rough hug.

"Now don't forget, look up old Fred day after tomorrow."

"I'll do that and thanks again."

Turning, he gave Bruno yet another last pat and started down the alley on his way to getting settled in his new accommodation. *What a laugh*, he thought, *my accommodation. Never mind, it's just a start.*

****

Alex stopped off at a little produce market en route. Impressed with the range of vegetables and fruit, he centred on the Cox's apples, familiar to him because they had been his mother's favourite. She'd told him that the apple was named after Richard Cox; the man who had first grown it in the early 1800s. He loved it as much as she had. Sweet and juicy, it was a crisp apple that always left a fresh taste in his mouth as if he'd just cleaned his teeth.

The man behind the counter smiled a toothless smile, having seen the boy eying the apples and just to get the 'lie of the land' Alex moved closer to engage him in conversation.

"Do you want to buy any then?"

"Oh, I'm just checking out the produce," Alex said casually. "Not really in the market today but I would be interested in any 'fallers' or ones that are already 'on the turn'. Maybe I can make some sort of a deal when I drop by again."

The man couldn't fail to notice how poor and thin the boy was, he already had the picture; the youngin was as hungry as he looked, gaunt with not a spare bit of fat on his bones. He piled a few apples in a bag with a couple of pears.

Alex, watching him, rushed on with his carefully prepared spiel.

"If you ever need any help I'm right handy and can turn my hand to most things. I'll even clean up around the stalls. Maybe I could work for anything you give me."

Handing over the bag, the man spoke softly and Alex picked up a slight Irish accent.

"Now look, lad, I'm here seven days a week and if you don't see me just ask any of my mates for Arnie, I'll be around somewhere nearby."

Alex clutched his bag of goodies thinking what with the bakery and some produce once in a while from Arnie; he should be in good shape.

"Thanks a lot, do you want me to do a bit of a sweep around for you or anything?"

"No lad, be off, I'll put you to work next time you come."

Arnie grinned and in spite of his toughness, his heart went out to the boy who he knew was proud and hurting inside. He recognised all the signs having been down that road himself.

****

That afternoon was tough for Alex. His knapsack was weighing him down but he was determined to keep it with him, never to lose sight of it. He had to find somewhere for the night fairly close to Primrose Hill and the burnt building. It was dusk by the time he reached the general area and an eerie mist was closing in. He guessed that Regents Park and the canal would not be far, adding to the lack of visibility. Getting about would be much easier once he was more familiar with the tube train but at this point, he had to hang onto every bit of cash so he would be moving about on foot whenever he could.

Exhausted, he decided to rest up in a mini-park en route. As it was now dusk, he wouldn't have to wait long before the place was deserted. Moving slowly, he scanned the area for a suitable spot. A willow tree, great, there had to be water around, willows needed a lot of water for survival and this was a huge one. He cast around and sure enough there was a little stream nearby; perfect.

That night, glancing around surreptitiously to make sure nobody saw him, he entered the tree through the trailing boughs. What a perfect spot, clean, dry, quiet. He'd be able to keep his clothes clean and the birds would wake him at dawn. He could nip down to the stream for a quick splash and be on his way. Actually, this spot may prove better than Primrose Hill, although he should have several stopping off points for emergencies, he was thinking and anyway he didn't want to be seen in the same spot every night; it wouldn't take long for people to catch on.

Settling himself down, he got out his torch, making sure that he was in the thickest part of the tree, so that his light would not be seen from the outside. Propping it up, he kept it on just as long as he needed to eat a delectable lunch which he had saved especially for dinner. Bob had really done him proud with huge sandwiches that would hardly fit in his mouth, scrumptious apple pie and some fruit. Breakfast had been so hearty that he didn't really have any major hunger pangs, until then when he realised he was ravenous. While checking through his knapsack, he came across an envelope with Frank's writing on it. 'Just a little something to see you on your way lad, you take care of yourself and see you soon.' Inside the envelope was a wad of notes, Alex was bug-eyed, he would never have imagined how kind people could be to him. He'd spent so long expecting the worst and here he had received nothing but the best since taking to the streets. Well-fed and relatively calm, after all he was now a man of means; he fell into the deepest sleep, fortunately, once again without any demons to torture him.

The next morning, he was awakened suddenly by the trilling of birds. Any other time, he would have bristled but this morning, he was grateful. Among his possessions, he had a very old-gold watch which had belonged to his father, given to him with great ceremony by his mother.

"This watch was very special to your father; he would have wanted you to have it. It was given to him by his mother when she lost her husband, your grandfather, in WW1. It had belonged to your grandfather and was presented to him by his colleagues from Walls Meat Company because of his years of service, which ended when he went into WW1 to fight for all of us just like your father did. Walls had been forced to lay off workers every summer because people didn't eat so much meat in the warm weather, I suppose. Anyway, sales dropped but your grandfather was retained because he had been with the company for so long. It wasn't until after WW1 that the company started making ice cream and they became rich and famous throughout the world and you know how good the ice cream is, don't you?"

Then she ruffled his hair and smiled down at him.

Alex truly valued his special gift and kept it in the little tin with his other possessions that he could not afford to lose.

Getting it from his knapsack, he noted that the time was a little after 5:00 and after winding it up carefully replaced it. He'd better get cracking while the place was still deserted. He chose a shrubby area by the stream, stripped off and submerged himself as it was just deep enough to cover him sufficiently if he lay down in the cool water and boy was it cool. After the initial shock, he found it so invigorating that he almost purred with pleasure. He had the remains of a soap bar and deftly soaped himself. Handling the bar with caution as he wanted it to last as long as possible, he quickly put it back in its container. His mum was obsessively clean and had instilled good hygiene and good manners into her son. *Me mam would be proud of me*, he thought, squeezing his eyes against the emergent tears that again threatened to overtake him. He hastened his drying with one of the two old coloured towels. His mother had used them on him when he was little which now seemed a lifetime ago and he felt a strong attachment to them. Burying his face in the pure cotton, he indulged in a few moments imagining she was with him. He could almost smell her sweet fragrance in the towel just like the freesias she had always loved; they had always been her favourite flowers.

"Okay, that's enough of that," he muttered.

Once fully clothed, he felt much better and confident to face the day. He had saved a little bread and fruit for breakfast and gulped it down with water from the stream. Knapsack on back, he carefully parted the boughs and noting there were still no people around, slipped briskly out of the tree and set out on his way, stopping to fill his water bottle en route. Yes, this would make a really good spot for him to stay.

****

He was looking for Sid's bakery, Frank's contact and he wanted to do it first while he was still fresh and clean looking, had to make a good impression. The bakery was located near Primrose Hill and would be perfect as he hoped to make that area his base.

Just as Frank had said, he found Sid to be very friendly and welcoming.

"Come on in me boy, I've been waiting for you for the last couple of days. I've got some goodies for you and your mam. Elsie," he shouted, "Alex is here."

Alex was taken aback and noting his incredulous expression, Sid carried on hardly pausing for breath.

"Yes, Frank told me how you and your mam had fallen on bad times and would I look out for you. Well lad, any friend of Frank's is a friend of mine and you stop by regular and I'll always have a little something for you both. It may be yesterday's but all my stuff keeps well."

Still, the boy looked like a deer caught in headlights and Sid further elaborated.

"And another thing, Frank has been good to me over the years, a real mate and I can't tell you how great it is for me to be able to help out people he cares about.

Have you had anything to eat today? I've got a drop of really good oxtail soup and fresh warm bread. Now how does that grab you?"

Alex's mouth fell open. In the last couple of days, he'd met more kind people coming forward to help than he had in his entire life. Good old Frank for keeping his secret.

Elsie came bustling in. She was a large woman with pink cheeks and a huge crisp-white apron tied around her ample body with a huge bow. Alex thought she looked like a ship in full sail.

"Oh just look at you lad, you look half starved. Let's get some food in you."

Alex sat down to another robust meal with good company. He had begun to realise just how blessed Frank was to have such friends and how he enjoyed their company. There had been so many times when he had felt so utterly alone.

Having finished, he sat back and met Sid's scrutiny, hoping he hadn't shown just how hungry he was. The last thing he wanted was for Sid to know he was an orphan living on the street, although he was twelve now, going on thirteen, not a kid any more, he'd be a grown man soon.

"Just want to tell you, sir."

"You call me Sid lad, like everyone else does."

"Well Sid, just want you to know if ever you need any help in the shop or the storeroom or anywhere, I'm pretty handy and would be glad to work for food any time."

Sid beamed, “Well yeah I’ll take you up on that but you’ll get your grub and a few pence if you do anything for me. Got it?”

“Yes sir, I mean Sid.”

“Actually, I do have a little something. Frank tells me you’re very mechanical and can get into locks and all sorts. Well today, I managed to lock myself out of the store room. Would that be something in your area of expertise, young man?”

“Right on the money,” Alex hoped he sounded grown up. “Show me where the room is.”

Confronted by the door, he took a series of wires out of his pocket and a small piece of metal, almost like the lead in a very fine pencil with grooves on it. He fiddled around for a few minutes working on the lock.

“Open sesame,” he said with a cheeky grin spread all over his face and they both found themselves looking through into the store room from the open door.

“Well, I’ll be damned. Aren’t you the clever one?”

“How far is Primrose Hill or Regents Park from here?” Alex spoke nonchalantly as if what he’d just accomplished was nothing.

“I’d say about a twenty-five minute walk. If you’re going by tube it’s just a few minutes to Chalk Farm and the same to Primrose Hill. Actually, the walk from Chalk Farm is not bad at all.”

They were at the door by now.

“Now don’t forget lad, usually if you drop by early morning, you’ll get yesterday’s leftovers. If you drop by later, you’ll get this morning’s left overs.”

“Me mam thanks you Sid.”

“Oh God bless him, poor little lad.”

Elsie smothered him in hugs and he thought he would actually stop breathing, so buried was he in that ample body. She smelt good though just like fresh baked bread.

They had done him proud. He was weighed down with the weight of the bag as he went down the road humming.

"Me mam always said I had the luck of the Irish. I suppose I do have Irish somewhere in me. Seems to me they're everywhere, in the pubs, down in the docks, yep, reckon I've got Irish running through me veins."

****

Frank, Bob, Sid and Elsie were to become the mainstay of his existence; without them, he would have perished for sure.

Chapter 5
Alex Sets His Routine on Streets

Alex decided to walk from Chalk Farm to Primrose Hill as he wasn't one hundred percent sure of the exact location of the bombed building but the remains of a huge red brick building stood out in his memory and he knew he would be able to find it again. Maybe it had been a boys' home at one time. He cringed at the thought. Boys' home, that would be ironical to wind up living in a disused boys' home after all his efforts to avoid it. Trudging along the road and beginning to feel somewhat desolate, he wondered if he should come clean with Bob and throw himself on his mercy. Well, he'd have a shot at making it on his own before he did that, he decided. Once he'd worked with Bob and they really got to know each other, things might be different.

The road looked vaguely familiar to him and suddenly there it was; unchanged and just as daunting. He knew of one entrance hidden behind the coal bunker and he was pretty sure there was another behind a barberry bush around the back if it was still there. That would be his choice because from what he remembered, it led directly into the basement which should be relatively undamaged by the bombing. That entrance had the added advantage that he would be able to squirm his way around the treacherous thorns of the barberry. Being lithe and slim, he would succeed but it would be a major deterrent to anybody else who might have the same idea.

Following a quick reconnaissance of the outer structure, he was delighted to see the bush was still there only much bigger and after a cursory glance around, he squeezed behind it. Sure enough, there was a small hatch, which he was just able to get through.

"Well, I'd better get my act together soon, because it'll not be long before I'm too big to get through this hole," he muttered aggravated and stressed that he would ruin his clothes as he dusted himself down. It was imperative that he didn't look like what he was, a street waif.

The basement was perfect as he had suspected. There were a couple of small window slits with bars across and overall the rooms were pretty clean, all things being considered. He tracked down the stairs leading to the upper floor noting they were quite badly damaged. It was essential there was no entry from above so he ascended gingerly to the door at the top. Joy oh joy, the key was still in the lock and although difficult to turn, with the use of a little of his own lock oil he was able to lock it from the inside as he would have no need to go into the upper reaches and wanted to make absolutely sure that nobody could get down to the lower level. Having ascertained that there was just the one entrance, the one which he'd used, he felt a little more secure. In the event of an emergency, he reckoned he could exit through one of the bigger windows; there were two which seemed a little frail compared to the others and he could use his wrench on the rusted out bars.

A few hours' work gave him a much better sense of the place. After all, he only wanted it for sleeping and resting up. Having cleaned up the old wooden cot, he figured it would make a reasonable bed. He could get something in the form of a bed roll from the second-hand shop later. Leaving stealthily, he was satisfied that his future living accommodation was workable. Of course, he'd always carry his valuables with him and only leave superfluous stuff behind as he moved about.

He stopped off in the little park with the willow tree for a bite to eat and freshen up in the stream as he entered the Regents Park and Primrose Hill area, and soon came across his 'money' tree thinking he would deposit the tin and some more cash. He shinned up it quite easily. The hole was even better than he remembered and would keep his belongings completely dry.

The rest of the day was taken up with exploring the outskirts of Regents Park, the canal and Primrose Hill Park. Meandering down the street, his eye fell on a little second-hand shop tucked in tightly amongst other little businesses. The huge range of goods really impressed him and taking his time he scrutinised everything carefully, fully aware he too was being scrutinised in case he pocketed anything. Certainly there was everything in stock that he would need and more; something for every occasion it seemed. The old man who ran the shop was very kind once he knew the boy had honest intentions and gave him a really good deal on the last bed roll. What a steal, Alex was thinking as he affixed it to his knapsack.

On his way back to the bombed building, he stopped at the far end of the stream in the little park and filled his water container. This end of the park was closer to the building and would be a shorter distance to carry water. Evening was drawing in and he reached his destination in half light. That night he slept well, feeing very secure in his new accommodation.

****

By the time he got to Earls Court station the next day, there was a fine drizzle falling which he knew could get depressing; thank goodness he had found somewhere dry to sleep. Fred wasn't hard to spot as Bob had said. He gave a cheery wave to which Fred responded smiling broadly.

"Ow yer doing then? You must be the lad Bob was on about."

"Yes sir, Bob tells me you have the details of my next assignment."

Alex hoped he sounded sophisticated, a man of the world.

"You got that right. Just give me a few minutes to sell the rest of the 'Morning Edition' and we'll pop up the road for some breakie and discuss business."

Alex pulled his cap down further over his ears against the drizzle and squatted down next to Fred under the canopy. It was essential to keep himself and his clothes as dry as possible. His mum had warned him about hanging around in damp or wet clothes. "That's where the colds came from," she always said and he couldn't afford to get sick, not now, not right at the start of his career.

He liked Fred who obviously reciprocated and as they ate their breakfast in the little café, Alex felt quite at home. George, the owner was a long-standing friend of Fred's and was very generous with their eggs and bacon, and with the bill, as Alex found out when he was counting out his money.

"Put that away lad, it's on the house," was the almost irritated retort he got from the big man in the apron. Alex felt obliged to repay the gesture.

"Thanks very much and if you ever need me to do any jobs for you, I'm right handy with locks, cash tills, in fact just say the word if you have anything you need doing or fixing. I'm your man. I'll be in here with Fred quite regular."

He looked at Fred for reassurance and confirmation which he got, along with a knowing wink, directed at both him and George.

"Well young man, I'll keep that in mind. I should have some jobs for you from time to time. Now do you want refills or anything else?"

Alex thought he'd died and gone to heaven.

****

His assignment was for the next night. He was to meet Charlie, Bob's contact and his mate at a warehouse in the city centre; they needed him to crack a lock which had proved impenetrable for both men. After they had gained entry and completed their tasks, he was to return the lock to its unopened state. Alex thought it would be a real feather in his cap if he could achieve what they couldn't.

After the job was done, they would be giving him either an envelope or package to take back to Bob. That would be terrific because he could spend the night at the old theatre and visit Frank the next morning before he hooked up with Bob. Yes, that would work really well.

After a shaking of hands, he bade Fred goodbye and both looked forward to their next get-together which by all accounts was not too far off.

****

Sid and Elsie gave Alex the usual warm welcome and fed him well when he called in later that day. He did a few jobs for Sid and repaired Elsie's old treadle sewing machine, for which she was eternally grateful. Sid was beaming broadly.

"See, I told you he was a clever lad."

Once again Alex left with a knapsack that he could hardly hoist up on his back and enough food to feed an army. By this time, the drizzle had turned to light rain and he was anxious to get himself bedded down for the evening. *Must get more batteries when I'm at Bob's, the torch light is getting a bit dim*, he thought, he made a mental note on his 'to do' list as he drifted off to sleep that night.

****

The next day found him at Frank's who was overjoyed to see him and once the preliminaries were through, Alex got straight to the point.

"Do you have any jobs for me?"

"Yep, made a list if you want to work through it."

Alex glanced over it and was pleased to see that the items listed were a piece of cake for him; every job was dead easy. He enjoyed his day with Frank and was glad he could help out. He knew the old man was getting on and his arthritis was impeding him in many ways. When he left, he knew he'd have to stop off at the theatre before he went on to the job. Once again the knapsack was too heavy. He couldn't take it like that to work, it was essential to travel light. Deciding to lighten the load a little, he entered his city residence and reorganised his knapsack, preparing food and clothes for his evening's return after meeting with Charlie.

The job went well that night, very smooth without incident. Alex was through the lock in less than a minute; both men looked at each other and back at the boy with admiration if not a little sheepishly as it had proved beyond their capabilities. Alex did his disappearing act and melded into the shadows while he waited for them to come out which was in short order. As always, anxious to get going, he demanded Bob's 'return on investment' while he restored the lock to its original state.

Clutching his package, he disappeared down the back streets like grease lighting and didn't breathe easily until he was back in the theatre. Upon opening his food package from Frank, he came across another little envelope once again a generous offering from his benefactor. *Boy, I may have to get that bank account opened sooner than I expected,* he thought. *That tin isn't going to hold too many more of these rolls of notes.*

****

The next day as Alex approached Bob's front door, it burst open and he noticed with amusement that Bob was hastily hustling a very nice looking woman onto the pavement. Her dress resplendent tripped the fine line between decadence and flamboyance. Bob was covered in embarrassment exacerbated by Alex's cheeky wink.

"What are you ogling at boy, aren't I allowed friends? This is Cathy. Cathy this is Alex."

Bob was making a valiant effort to bring some composure into the proceedings but knew he'd been well and truly nabbed. It wasn't far past sunup and lady friends would normally be at home in their own beds at this time.

"Nice to meet you young man, Bob has told me lots of good stuff about you," and turning to Bob, "Bob don't forget about Friday. I'll meet you at the pub."

Cathy's bright and friendly personality more than made up for any shortcomings in her dress sense, a style unto her own. Then she was gone, her delightful perfume pervading the air.

Bob met Alex's penetrating intense gaze.

"Yes, that's my friend Cathy, I've known her for years, we're really good friends."

"Yes, I gathered that."

Alex was really sticking his neck out just begging for a clip round the ear for his insolence but he was having too much fun and anyway Bob was now much more interested in the package that he was digging out of his knapsack. Positively snatching it from Alex, he disappeared into the back regions, only to appear shortly after grinning all over his face.

"That's for you boy and welcome to the team."

Alex was grinning all over his face too when he saw what was in his envelope and continued to do so all through their meal, even when Bob got launched on one of his political diatribes.

"And I don't know if you've heard or been following this nuclear debacle but they've just announced that we've got a nuclear bomb, you can bet it's only to compete with the Ruskies. Well, we're well and truly in it now. You mark my word, this is the start of the cold war. Wouldn't you think they've had enough of it, two wars since 1914? The country's only just beginning to recover from the last lot and they're at it again."

Alex was listening with half an ear, busily planning his routine as he wouldn't be reporting to Fred for a couple of days. He would definitely call on Arnie at the market. Maybe do a few jobs and stock up on produce. He also thought he might look Dan up as it was ages since he had seen him.

****

Such was the routine for the next couple of years. Bob never asked him about his mother and Alex suspected that he knew he had been fed a load of codswallop regarding Alex and his mum moving back together. Alex did wonder; however, what Bob must be thinking about how he was living but the subject was never raised.

Bob had given him the use of his loft to sleep over when timing between jobs got erratic and when an assignment was in the area. Alex had another growth spurt and thought he'd better do something about the 'money tree' situation. His last trip to the tree had been rather nostalgic for Alex and after retrieving his personal stash, his feet firmly on the ground, he laid his hands on the bark of the trunk.

"Thank you, tree, you've served me well but I'm almost a man now, too old and too big to climb you anymore."

His hands felt warm against the bark, almost as if he could feel the life of the great tree pulsating up the trunk.

Bob had been only too pleased to let him use the pawnshop address for convenience and helped him to open his first bank account. A sizeable sum was deposited to open the account. Bob was impressed, giving Alex one of his familiar winks.

That day was memorable. When they left the bank they jostled and played around all the way up the street, bonding in friendship with an ice cream each.

"I'm a man of means, thanks to you. I'm the rich kid on the block."

"That you are lad, that you are and there's more in the pot at the end of the rainbow."

Chapter 6
The First Meeting

Alex was in his 15th year and knew he should be 16 to apply for a social security number, which he was going to do, as that was the only way to earn real money. A permanent address and an employer would be required to complete the forms so he resolved to sit down with Bob and ask him if he would help him out so that everything was legal.

Cripes, he thought, *I suppose I'll have to come clean at that time and spill the beans about how I've been living. One thing's for sure, everything is going to be in order so that I can't be forced back to the authorities and shipped out of the country.*

He went back into the city fairly regularly on jobs for Bob, although he was still based in Primrose Hill. The burnt building had been his home off and on for more than two years now, along with a couple of emergency stop overs, as he called them. When he was in the centre doing jobs for Bob, he still stayed in the old theatre overnight which was much the same as when he and Dan had played there. It was one of those old buildings that everybody seemed to have forgotten about. His 'quarters' were quite liveable now that he had furnished them with a few basic necessities and quite comfortable considering the circumstances.

Since opening his bank account, Alex had accrued an impressive amount; every pound he could spare went into the bank and the clerk had set him up with a little record book so that he could see his total increase with every deposit he made. He was filled with pleasure as he watched it grow. Grinning wryly at the last deposit, the thought crossed his mind of an old man still climbing the tree to get his stash. Bob had been really terrific in helping him out and had personally accompanied him to the bank to open the account.

Frank was always glad to see him. Alex was sad to see his old friend was definitely showing signs of age although always appeared young at heart. He put him at somewhere around 70 or more. It was hard to pin point his exact age because he still had a full head of hair only flecked with grey. Frank still loved his bakery and all his customers kept him on his toes. They had been regulars for years and the business was mostly through word of mouth. Alex would remember the vanilla slices for as long as he lived, light and fluffy layered pastry squares stuffed with jam and cream, and topped with an icing sugar glaze and when dairy was in short supply, the bread pudding full of raisins and spices was out of this world. A slice of that would carry him all day. Frank's prices were good too, so he was never short of customers.

Whenever Alex worked at night away from Bob's, he continued to stay overnight in the old theatre if it was reasonably close or if not, a bombed tenement building or disused warehouse were always places where he could avoid the other street people. He was aware there was always the chance of running into acquaintances and other boys who had been orphaned as he was, running wild to escape the authorities. The city was full of them; he had to watch himself that was for sure. Alex knew he could stay with Frank and did on some occasions but he had to have some very good reason for working at night, so on those occasions he stayed on the street and that night was one such occasion.

He had to meet a buddy of Bob's in the alley behind an antique shop. There was a safe to be cracked and they knew Alex was just the boy for the job. As always, casting around in all directions, he entered the alley. About halfway down he came upon two men in an alcove. He knew Charlie but not the other man and regarded him suspiciously as he did all strangers. He would get the job done and get out of there pronto he decided.

"Come on then let's get a move on. Where is it?"

Feeling a little unnerved at the presence of a stranger, his voice sounded strange even to him, as if his tongue had dried out and was too big for his mouth.

The stranger stepped aside and Alex spotted a safe which, to his relief, had a locking mechanism which was very familiar to him.

"Keep your mouths shut and your eyes open for the bobbies, I need to concentrate."

Having directed the gormless pair, he then crouched down and lovingly fingered the combination lock, as if he were about to unwrap a special gift package. Backwards and forwards he went and after about five minutes a smile broke loose on his lips and the contents of the safe were displayed.

Alex had long since learned to keep his mouth zipped and ask no questions when he was called upon for these types of jobs, so he got straight to business.

"Where's the envelope for Bob? I've got to get going he's expecting me."

Charlie handed it to him and after bidding them a goodnight, he melted into the murky shadows of the alley, momentarily pausing to stash the envelope into his knapsack. He then made his way stealthily to the old theatre down the back streets which he knew so well.

Hearing a sob he froze and there she was, the most beautiful girl he thought he had ever seen. Hard to say how old she was but she couldn't have been more than 15 years. Crouched with her arms round her knees, she rocked backwards and forwards in despair, wretched and frozen. Taking off his jacket, he put it round her shoulders and wrapped his arms around her holding her close to him until her shaking subsided. Gradually he released her when he thought she was warm enough and smiled to give her confidence.

"What's your name then?"

"Amy, my name's Amy."

"Well Amy, I'm Alex. What are you doing here?"

"I left home some months ago; lost track of exactly when. It was just my mum and I when I was growing up; my dad left us when I was very young. Then she got herself a new boyfriend and that was okay with me, she needed someone to take her mind away from the rotten treatment she'd received from my father but then her boyfriend moved in with us. They hadn't known each other long but he had money and set us up in a lovely little house near the New Forest in Hampshire. Things were okay for a while but he never really liked me, my mum was always trying to defend me but things were just getting worse; they were arguing about me being there. He seemed to watch me all the time and it got really uncomfortable. I was afraid to tell mum and knew it wasn't going to improve; I just felt in the way all the time, so I made plans to get out. I didn't want to go, I loved that house and the garden was a paradise on earth. I had savings for school but it's all gone now and I've nowhere to live, been living on the streets." She started to cry again, long anguished sobs and frantically dabbed her eyes with a bit of rag which she managed to drag out of her pocket.

"Do you have anything to eat in that bag?"

Alex dived into his faithful knapsack and gave her a sandwich. Frank had been especially generous and had given Alex such a huge sack of food he had trouble fitting it all in.

"Quick, get that down you and I'll take you somewhere safe for the night but you have to give me your word you'll never ever mention this place to anybody."

Even though they had just met she seemed familiar and her vulnerability was bringing out a strong sense of protection within him. She nodded and he took this to be her word.

They arrived at the old theatre and entered through the hidden entrance. He led her through a maze of corridors, a particularly circuitous route for added security just in case and eventually through a door at the end. Standing in a very large room, Alex headed over to a disused cabinet and pulled it to one side, just enough for them to squeeze through into another room. Pulling it behind them, he could see Amy was impressed, her eyes were everywhere.

"My goodness you've certainly got yourself fixed up, haven't you?" She was incredulous.

"This place looks like a good hotel room. What's in here?"

It was a bathroom of sorts. The appliances were cracked and worn but the sink and toilet were still intact.

"The council have forgotten to turn off the water so I usually fill that bucket and manage to get a good wash. Not sure I want to drink the water though. I carry mine from the tap up the alley at the back of the second hand shop. I know the merchant as I buy the odd thing from him now and then."

He started preparing the table for them to have something to eat while he spoke, delving into his bag at intervals.

He saw that she was in rough shape and handed her his water bottle watching her eagerly gulping it back choking in her haste. He wondered when she had last eaten or drunk anything decent.

They both devoured their food and finished off with some fruit and water, only pausing once in a while for a little conversation. Once their meal was finished, there was no stopping them and their chatter was non-stop. Neither could believe how well they got along and how much they seemed to have in common.

Finally, Alex stood. They were both showing signs of sheer exhaustion and always cognisant of timing, he started clearing away the remnants of their meal.

"Now do you want to get cleaned up and I'll dig up a blanket for you?"

When she reappeared, he settled her down on an old straw mattress with the blanket.

"Where are you sleeping?"

Alex had been wondering the same thing.

"Don't worry your head about me, I'll sort myself out."

He grabbed the other blanket and after a good swish down, settled on the old carpet. What was he going to do with her, he wondered? He had to get back to Bob's with his envelope and pick up his own 'donation to the cause'. Suddenly having a brainwave, he thought of good old Frank. *Yes, I'll take her to Frank and see if she can stay with him for a couple of days until I get back. That would give us a chance to think things out. She can't stay on the streets by herself she's not going to make it.* He couldn't imagine how she'd made it this far. He would broach the subject to her in the morning.

He'd just managed to drift off into sleep when halfway through the night, she leapt on him terrified and half out of her mind with fear it seemed.

"Are there any rats here? Please let me sleep with you."

She was frantically trying to get under his blanket. *This is getting a bit much*, he thought, struggling to his feet.

"Now get back on that mattress. I've got to get some sleep we've got an early start in the morning."

"Only if you stay with me, I'm scared," she wailed.

"Oh for Christ's sake; sorry but you really bring out the worst in me."

He climbed in beside her and she fell asleep almost immediately. Feeling very uncomfortable, both physically and emotionally, he was afraid to move in case he woke her.

****

What a rotten night that was, he thought as he struggled to his feet in the morning. He hadn't closed his eyes and his skin felt like sandpaper.

"Well, that was the best sleep I've had in a while," she said stretching luxuriously some time later.

"Good. I'm glad somebody slept well," he said sourly.

He had already carried out all his ablutions and gone up to the water tap for fresh water and filled the pitcher. He'd got used to moving about in the early hours while all the deadbeats were sleeping off the previous night's debauchery. He laid out some more of Frank's food on the makeshift table, while Amy was sorting herself out.

“We have to get out of here soon while the place is deserted.”

He was eying the rough jeans that only an orphaned waif would wear, but her pretty little pink blouse really suited her.

“I’m going to take you to a friend of mine. You don’t have to worry, he’s an absolute gentleman. My mother and I knew him as far back as I can remember but you have to look like you’re not on the streets, or he’ll worry and wonder what is going on. Right now, you look like you fit right in. Do you have anything else to wear? I don’t want to lie to Frank. I’m just going to say that you are a friend who needs a place to stay for a couple of days. Frank will be good with that and if you behave yourself, I’ll pick you up when I’m back in the city in four days.”

He knew he had another assignment coming up from Bob not far from this area.

“Thank you, oh thank you.”

“Yeah, yeah I just don’t know what to say.” Alex was mimicking her throwing in all her mannerisms which he knew inside out already.

Sitting across from him after she had changed into another pair of pants only marginally more presentable, she reached across and touched his hand lightly.

“You saved me, you are my king and I thank you, kind sir.”

He almost choked on his bread; it was so eerie.

“My mum always called me that. She named me after Alexander the Great and always said I was her little king.”

“Well, you’re mine too, and look at this magic castle you’ve brought me to.”

Their peals of laughter echoed all around the empty room.

Chapter 7
Friends and Lovers

When they arrived at Frank's, he opened his eyes wide but managed to restrain himself and kept to the preliminary introductions.

"Frank, this is my friend Amy; she's in London for a short while and has been waiting for somebody to show up."

Somebody showed up alright, thought Alex, *and let's just hope Frank will put her up until I get back from Camden Town. Give me a chance to think this through.*

Amy held out her hand to Frank and he took it enthusiastically beaming with pleasure.

"Well Amy, I sure am glad to meet you. You must be exhausted moving through the city with Alex, he sure doesn't let the grass grow under his feet. Here I'll show you the bathroom if you want to freshen up."

As soon as they were on their own, Frank pounced on Alex.

"Where did you find this little princess? Come on lad fess up."

"Oh I just know her that's all." Alex smirked enjoying the attention.

"Well she's quite the little lady isn't she? Not from around here that's for sure."

"No, she came visiting from the south."

Alex was getting mildly uncomfortable.

"Do you think you could put her up for a few nights? She really does need somewhere to stay. Frank, I'll owe you one if you can watch out for her till I get back. I'm working for the bloke I told you about; you know the one who is a locksmith with the pawnshop. He'll be expecting me and I don't want to keep him waiting, hanging around with Amy for whoever is coming and they may not even show up and what then. She's better somewhere safe until I get back."

"Of course, lad no problem, no problem at all, she'll be okay here."

"I'll be back in the city in three or four days at the most."

Frank knew what the locksmith and pawnshop usually meant but said nothing. The boy looked as if he had landed square on his feet and he was proud of him as if he were his own.

"Any friend of Alex's is a friend of mine and adding grudgingly, I suppose I have to give up my room for princess, she's obviously a lady."

Amy appeared suddenly looking a little abashed.

"Oh no, I couldn't have you do that."

"Well, we can't have you sleeping on the sofa now, can we? The spare room is full of storage boxes. So that's that settled; now what about a bite to eat?" Frank changed the subject immediately, looking a little shamefaced at his imprudence.

"Alex can you fix the till? I'm having trouble with it again and I'll have to get hold of another one if you can't get it going."

A while later, all having practically inhaled a heart-warming meal and the till being fixed, Frank was eying both of them. He didn't want to be obvious but he was thinking, *cripes they're so young but they certainly make a pair, a good match.*

****

It was very early morning as Alex had to clear the centre before it really woke up. Frank and Amy gave him a good send off and Amy threw her arms around his neck as he was about to leave.

"You won't be long coming back for me, will you?"

"No, course not, we have things to sort out."

Smothered with embarrassment, especially when he got a very familiar wink from Frank, Alex busied himself getting his knapsack positioned on his back. Looking over his shoulder one last time, he saw Amy with her arm locked firmly around Frank's. Standing close to each other, they looked just like very old friends.

Hastening down the alley, he felt a strange sense of loss. He had enjoyed having her around and looking after her. *Idiot*, he thought, *haven't you got enough on without developing feelings for a slip of a girl for cripes sake, get your head together*? And he did. He didn't give Amy another thought, well hardly, until he arrived safely at his destination.

Bob was delighted with the envelope and reciprocated with one of his own for Alex.

****

Amy and Frank were getting on like a house on fire when Alex arrived back at the bakery a few days later and were heavily involved in the baking for the counter and café section. Frank was teaching her how to operate the huge ovens and use the various pieces of heavy-duty commercial equipment. Alex felt slightly left out as she was totally occupied and he didn't get the exuberant welcome he was expecting. But crikey didn't she look sweet with flour all over her nose and sporting an outsize pinafore type of apron that Frank had dug up from somewhere, probably his late wife's. She had been a fair sized woman according to what Alex's mother had told him. Frank was gently chastising her for doing something the wrong way.

"No princess, no that's not the right way to turn these sponge cakes, give me the spatula and I'll show you again. Here, now you try."

Eventually she got it right and Frank finally turned his attention to Alex.

"So, how are you doing lad?" Not waiting for an immediate reply, Frank proliferated.

"Have to say this little girl is a real tonic. She can stay with me any time. If you decide to stay in this part of town princess, I could use the help in the bakery."

Amy's face lit up.

"I'd like that Frank, I really would."

Later that night in the old theatre, they sat and talked.

"Amy, you'd do well to consider Frank's offer. You could stay with him and work in the bakery. At least it would get you off the streets. I can see he's really fond of you and you would be a great help to him not only in the business. You would be good company for him as well."

"I like Frank but I want to stay with you. I could always help Frank out and stay with him the odd night when you're not in the city."

Alex was flattered but still concerned.

"I think you'd be better staying at his place. This is not the way to live, particularly for a princess like you."

They were going to Bob's the next day so Alex let the subject drop for a while but Amy persisted.

"Look, after we get back from Bob's why don't we talk to Frank about me working with him for a bit and staying on the odd night? Do you think he'd go for that? I just want to be with you when you're around; after all you're my king."

"Yeah, Yeah, I know."

Throwing off his acute discomfort, he leapt up.

"I'll go and get some drinking water and you do what you need to while I'm gone and we'll get some sleep. We have to be up early tomorrow. You know the routine."

Later that night when they were settled, Alex was thinking, *she really is a little princess*, Frank named her well. As if she sensed him thinking of her, she turned to face him.

"Alex, can I be your girlfriend?"

"Well I'll have to think about that, I'll let you know. Now get some sleep."

His voice was crackly and rasping, exacerbated by the fact that he was drowning in hormones.

****

Hurrying down the street at sunrise the next day, they came in sight of Bob's.

"Oh my God, what's that?"

Amy clung to Alex as Bruno bore down on them in full flight. She got behind Alex as the massive brute slammed into them, knocking them both to the ground. Bob was at the doorway by then almost splitting his pants, doubled over he was laughing so hard.

"Bruno, get over here this minute you big bugger, you get over here."

The dog immediately left his fun and returned to his master, leaving the two teens to get up and collect themselves, falling over each other they were laughing so much.

Bruno couldn't resist another charge and once again tackled them both to the ground; just a mélange of legs, arms, fur and slobber. This time Bob was really firm and

Bruno half-heartedly swaggered back to him taking his own sweet time, leaving the pair once again getting themselves together. What fun, oh what a laugh they all had. Bruno was besotted with Amy. He couldn't stop licking her and constantly knocked her to the ground by accident. Bob always kept an eye on him though because Amy was such a slip of a girl, *so tiny and delicate but what a little beauty*, he thought echoing Frank's sentiments.

Later, following a hefty breakfast, Amy passed by them into the kitchen to wash the dishes, looking over her shoulder at both who obviously wanted to discuss 'stuff'.

"Why don't you two men discuss business while I go and clear up?"

Alex tried to look nonchalant about the 'men' bit but Bob looked at him knowingly.

"What a little sweetheart and looks like she's taken a shine to you alright," he said after Amy had left the room. "Now I believe you've got something for me."

Alex fished the envelope out of the knapsack and the usual routine ensued. Bob left hurriedly, to return shortly after, beaming all over his face as he handed an envelope to Alex, who just as furtively squirrelled it away making room for Bob on the sofa.

"Now Alex, my long-standing friend, Harry, skippers his own tug up and down the Thames, sometimes he does jobs off the estuary as well. I've been thinking about your situation and while I can keep you busy, I think we need to think in terms of a proper job for you. You're a growing lad and you need to focus on the future now and get something a bit more stable. He's in port for a couple of days and I want to introduce you to him. If things pan out, you might be able to start with him as a trainee when you're sixteen. There are so many different areas you could work in once you get the proper training. What do you think?"

"Oh boy, oh boy, thank you Bob. You know I love the water and being around boats. I would really like to meet him."

"Okay then, we'll do it tomorrow; Amy do you have a minute?"

Amy came out of the kitchen and Bob continued.

"Listen Amy, Alex and I have to discuss some business tomorrow with one of my mates. We'll only be a few hours. Can you amuse yourself while we're gone?"

"Of course I can," she said indignantly. "I'll wash my hair, do my nails and stuff when you're gone, and I'll be company for Bruno. Do you have anything you want me to do for you?"

That settled Amy and Alex made ready to leave.

"I just have to stop off at the bank." Alex said importantly.

"And then I'll take you to my country residence."

Amy raised her eyebrows.

"Is there no end to you and your box of tricks?"

The air rang with the sheer joy of their laughter and youth.

****

Once again Amy was impressed having slid easily behind the bush at the back of the old building and now stood in the basement.

"Well what do you think of the place?" Alex asked her later.

"Not as upmarket as your town residence but very impressive, not so keen about the lack of mod cons though."

“Never mind, you’ll enjoy your dip in the ice cold water of the stream at 5:00 tomorrow.”

He was laughing again.

“Can’t wait,” she was already drifting off to sleep.

****

The next morning brought them a warm and loving welcome from Sid and Elsie, particularly the latter who fussed around the young woman and whisked her away to talk girl talk.

“Oh well done lad, well done. What a little gem,” was all Sid kept saying.

Alex did a few jobs for Sid while Elsie sorted through some clothes with Amy, looking for a silk scarf she wanted the girl to have.

“Amy, are you ready? We have to get going. Don’t want to keep Bob waiting.”

Alex was moving towards the door and following hugs all round and admiration for the new scarf Amy was sporting, they were on their way.

Amy got the usual welcome from Bruno.

“He’s obviously been around men too much,” said Bob. “The hound is very obviously in love with the little lady.”

Both men noticed Bruno went a little easier on Amy now and contented himself with trying to lick her to death.

“Boy, don’t need a bath when I come here,” she said squealing with delight. Of course when the dog tried to sit with her on the sofa, that was a bit much and Bob had to intervene again.

****

Harry shook hands warmly with Alex as Bob introduced them and Alex felt the sheer strength of the man. His grip was enough to break a man's hand with one squeeze. He gave them a good tour of the vessel and explained the functions as he went along. Alex was hanging onto every word interjecting periodically with some very intelligent comments and questions. Harry was impressed, so much so that at the end of the tour he felt very comfortable with the youth.

"Do you think you would like to put in some time with me this year then?"

"That I would, sir."

Alex was over the hill with excitement.

"We'll see how you do lad and take it one step at a time. Now do you want to give us a few minutes, Bob and I have some things to discuss?"

After Alex had gone off to examine some life-saving equipment, Harry got down to it with Bob.

"He'll do very nicely Bob, it would be a pleasure to bring the boy up to speed. Did you hear his questions and comments? He's a smart one, real quick learner. I'd find him very useful and when he turns sixteen, he can come on-board officially."

****

It was 2nd June, 1953. Approximately three million people jostled and pushed each other to get a better view as they lined the streets of London. Alex, Amy, Dan and his girlfriend Rosalind were in amongst them. The king was dead and it was the day of the coronation of Queen Elizabeth II. What a magnificent procession of horses, coaches and Royals. The pomp and grandeur surpassed all other. The excitement bordered on hysteria as the crowds pressed against the police barriers to get closer.

Everybody was in awe and talked about it for months to come. The four teenagers had the time of their lives and concluded their day in a little café in Clapham before Amy and Alex took off back to town.

Alex and Dan had been basically joined at the hip since their first meeting, they were so close and the two girls hit it off from the time they were first introduced, even though there was mounting racialism in London at this time centred on the Caribbean immigrants. More than once Amy and Alex had borne the brunt of it when they were out with the two Jamaicans but this day had proved to be perfect and had gone smoothly without incident; a memorable occasion for all.

The friends got together as often as they could after that day; usually meeting up in coffee bars. Cappuccino had made its appearance at war's end and London's Soho became a mecca for coffee houses and bars providing forums for young enthusiasts to get together and air their views. From the artsy crowd to anti-nuclear activists, from the jazzers and budding rock and rollers to the beatniks, they were all 'soaking up the atmosphere' of youthful exuberance and opinions to share with would be supporters of their causes. The four fit right in offering their wholehearted support to the nuclear disarmament issue. Amy and Alex meshed particularly well with the beatniks sporting their bohemian style attire. Created more from necessity, their hit and miss style was as patrons of the second hand shop, rather than from calculated fashion sense of being right 'out there' and up to the minute when it came to the latest fashions.

****

Each exhilarating day rolled into the next. Alex became completely bowled over by Amy, believing himself to be in love. They still hadn't told anyone they were living on the streets and their biggest worry was to make sure their clothes were in good order. The owner of the second hand shop got to know them well and always held back the better clothes, giving them first option. So the two were able to keep themselves pretty well set up, in fact became quite stylish, which was just as well as they were moving in quite a social set with Dan and Rosalind whenever they had free time.

Alex wondered if Bob knew their situation, he came pretty close to the mark sometimes with his comments; a smart man but he never questioned them or got into their business until that fateful day.

Chapter 8
Confessions

"So what are we going to do Alex?"

Amy's face was pale and strained as they sat in the old theatre having just finished some of Frank's treats.

"How far along are you?"

"The doctor says about four months, the baby will be born in about five months, could be less."

Alex was silent as his brain tried to digest what she had just told him. She started crying. He couldn't bear it when she cried. His heart felt as if it was being ripped out of his chest.

"Don't cry Amy, I can't stand it, please don't cry. Let's just think this through and we'll decide what to do in the morning."

Alex was pleased to see that she was able to get some sleep that night, although he never closed his eyes. Finally throwing in the towel at 4:45, he got up and made a start on the day moving about quietly so as not to disturb Amy. Picking up the pitcher, he went for fresh water. She was up and readying herself when he got back but she remained silent and unapproachable.

Alex finally broke the silence when they had finished their meal.

"Amy, I propose that we throw ourselves on Bob's mercy. I'm sure he has an idea of how we are living and the sooner we get it all out in the open, the better."

Amy fiddled around with a paper napkin on the table, refusing to look at Alex.

Frustrated, he made a move to clear things away.

"So that's settled then. We'll get our stuff together and head out. You'll not be staying here anymore; it's not fit for you in your condition. Bob will know what's best."

****

Bob was surprised to see them so early. They weren't expected until later in the day and judging by Amy's pale face and the obvious atmosphere, his chest tightened, fearing the worst.

"Right then," he said shoving the ghastly thought out of his mind.

"I'll get something for us to eat and you two can tell me what's going on."

Amy's eyes were downcast and Alex was sullenly shuffling his feet around. Even Bruno sensed something was brewing.

Going off to the kitchen, Bob was glad of a few minutes to collect himself.

Alex left nothing out from the time he had found his mum dead. How he had been living, how he had met Amy, leaving the latest development to last as Bob interjected.

"Why in God's name didn't you tell me? You know you could live with me anytime. There's that huge loft just going to waste."

"I was afraid to put you on a spot with the authorities. It's been my biggest dread that they'll catch me and ship me off to God knows where."

His voice petered out to just a squeak.

"Well by God, things are going to be different from now on."

Alex looked as if he were about to vomit.

"But that's not all is it?" Bob knew his fears were coming to fruition.

"No, it isn't and yes things are different. Amy's having a baby in about five months."

"Bloody hell; well you've really dumped yourselves in it now, haven't you?"

Bob turned towards the door groping for one of his rare cigarettes.

"You two don't move, I've got to get some air and my thoughts around this."

Amy remained unmoving, except to snatch her hand away from Alex when he tried to hold it.

Upon his return, Bob's heart went out to the teens. A spectre of hopelessness hung over their bowed heads; both just about as wretched as they could be.

"The first thing we're going to do is get in touch with Amy's mother and tell her the situation. You will both stay here for the time being and assuming she's prepared to help, we'll get Amy back down to Southampton a little later on, say a couple of months from now, that will give her mother a chance to get used to the idea."

Both of them nodded in agreement.

"Now about the sleeping arrangement, Alex you take the loft, and if I catch you trying to get into that girl's knickers again, you're out on your ear. Is that clear?"

Alex nodded not daring to open his mouth.

"Amy I'll make up the little room at the back for you for a few days. We'll go to Frank and put him in the picture so that you can continue to work in the bakery and it'll be better for you to live on the job, not so taxing for you until you're due to go south. A little work will help you stay focussed. Mark my words, the same thing applies to you though, they'll be no more hanky panky, got it?"

Amy nodded her agreement and like Alex, afraid to speak, averted her eyes while Bob continued, "And as we all need a little time to digest this, I'll contact your mother in the morning."

Following the initial shock, Amy's mother agreed to come up to London under the guise of a shopping spree as she didn't want her partner involved at this point, particularly as there was no love lost between him and her daughter.

****

The day of her mother's visit saw Amy in a state of rising hysteria.

"Don't worry I'll be there as referee. It'll be alright."

Bob had fully recovered and was thinking clearly. The young woman clung to his arm; he had been so good to them now that the shock waves had died down a bit.

They had arranged to meet Sylvia, Amy's mother, in a neutral spot, her hotel. Bob thought they would all be a little more at ease in new surroundings.

As they approached the hotel, Amy pointed out her mother sitting in the lounge. In spite of the situation, the older woman's smile was friendly as she extended her hand.

"Hello I'm Sylvia, Amy's mother and you must be Alex and Bob. I'm pleased to meet you both and Bob thank you for all your help."

Once they were settled at their table, Sylvia spoke quietly.

"So Amy, I have had a chance to think about this dilemma. There's a nice private facility not too far from the house where I think you should have the baby. I took the liberty of booking you in tentatively based on the timing Bob gave me. It's a lovely old rambling building, set in beautiful grounds. Your last few weeks before the baby comes should be calm and tranquil without any confrontation. I'll work on Bill in the meantime. He's not a bad man, you know it's just that you two don't see eye to eye.

Now the hard part, I'm sure both of you realise that you are ill-equipped to handle a baby; you are almost children yourselves which means that somebody has to step in. I won't see one of the family farmed out so the only solution is for me to adopt the child or at least be its legal guardian. Now should that be the case both of you would have to be out of the picture. We can't have a 'tug of war' situation and a child needs a controlled, secure environment to grow up in. Bob, what's your viewpoint?"

Bob was impressed with Sylvia's pragmatic approach to these dire circumstances and chose his own words carefully.

"I totally agree. These two have made a huge mistake but they need to get on with their lives. I have to say to both of you at this time that you're very fortunate to have this lady prepared to take the load."

Their eyes were fastened on the young pair.

"Perhaps you both want to take a walk and mull things over. Sylvia and I will get some refreshments ordered up while we're waiting for your comments and any questions."

****

The arrangements were put in place as outlined by Sylvia. Amy was to present herself one month before the baby was due, all being well and she would be placed in the facility. When the baby was born, the paperwork would be completed and Amy would leave as soon as she was fit.

Bob shook Sylvia's hand firmly as they readied themselves to leave.

"We'll stay in touch, and Alex and I will bring Amy down south when the time comes. Don't worry I'll see that everything is under control and that she is well looked after."

Sylvia had a tight rein on herself, appearing calm, collected and on top of events but they did see her reach for her handkerchief as she ascended the stairs to her hotel room.

****

In the weeks that followed, Alex resumed his work on the tugs and Amy returned to Frank's. It had been more than a little tense following the initial meeting with Frank but he thought the world of Amy, and was prepared to give her a leg up and keep an eye on her. Bob breathed a sigh of relief because he knew the kids would be vulnerable before and after the birth and at least Amy had some kind of a routine in the offing, with the added advantage that it gave her and Alex their sorely needed space from each other.

****

The weeks sped by and before they knew it, they were celebrating both Amy's and Alex's sixteenth birthdays. They didn't have a big bash in view of the circumstances but marked the occasion by going to Frank's who was finding it more difficult to get around and definitely beginning to show signs of wear. He did manage to put up the most splendid cake for both of them; however and for a time, happiness permeated the air again with much lip smacking of pure joy at the sheer indulgence of the occasion. It was just like old times.

Shortly after Alex entered his sixteenth year, Bob assisted him in getting his National Insurance Card and number, and he was all set for a seafaring career. At the same time, he got Amy signed up in readiness for taking up her formal bakery apprenticeship with Frank.

Harry took Alex on the payroll as a full-time permanent staff member and he commenced his training immediately. Bob was relieved, particularly as he knew Alex would be fully occupied working, learning and taking exams, and generally moving towards his goal. *That's one hurdle out of the way*, he thought, *and who knows this might be the making of the boy*. Bob was absolutely right.

Chapter 9
The Birth

The three travelled by road to Southampton. The train trip was approximately two and a half hours but they thought Amy would be more comfortable in the car as she would be able to stretch out in the back and they would be making frequent stops along the way. Bob phoned Sylvia as they were nearing their destination and she met them at the nursing home. Amy's room was bright and sunny, overlooking the gardens. The house exuded former opulence being set in formal lawns and rose gardens. Enormous oak trees bordered the acreage; they must have been over one hundred years old. There was an air of quietude throughout the property which regal trees of such an age seemed to promote. Even Amy appeared to show enthusiasm which had not been evident in her for some time.

Saying goodbye was hard. Her eyes sought Alex's and they held each other, obviously neither wanted to let the other go. Finally, she turned and one of the nursing staff took over.

Bob and Alex had decided to stay for a few days; they wanted to see some of the New Forest where the horses and ponies roamed freely. Since the 1800s landowners in the forest, referred to as commoners had been granted free grazing rights for their livestock. This practice not only maintained the ecology and character of the area but also prevented it from overgrowing and becoming a dense and mature forest once again.

They had also heard much about the local so-called witch who, in fact, was a legend in her own time running a shop in one of the New Forest villages. Her reputation was that of a psychic and expert in esoteric matters and having lived with the gypsies, was well versed in the ways of the forest. Alex and Bob were fascinated with the whole subject and hoped they too would get a chance to see her with her pet jackdaw on her shoulder.

They sat one lunch time enjoying a pie and chips in one of the forest pubs. When they had first walked in, they were greeted with an abrasive 'fuck off' and looked around in amazement laughing their heads off trying to locate the source of the profanity. It didn't take them long. A series of metallic sounding chuckles broke out and another round of coarse vulgarity rang through the rafters. The culprit was a mynah bird, dark and glossy dancing up and down on his perch by the huge stone fireplace and with the foulest tongue they'd heard in a long time; certainly brought in the trade though. The pub was a popular stopping off point and the bird was well known throughout the New Forest, greeting every new customer entering the premises with the same diatribe. What a riotous lunch and what a tonic to have a change of focus for a while.

During their stay, they visited Lymington, a Georgian market town. They loved the nautical atmosphere and boating facilities. As always, there was an abundance of pubs and restaurants, cobbled streets and the Old Town Quay. The air was brisk as they sat overlooking the water at Lymington just soaking up the atmosphere. The sea had an opalescent quality and even though the day was cloudy and overcast, a watery sun was making feeble attempts to peek through the clouds, and thousands of gem stones and diamonds marched spasmodically on the sway.

"You know, Bob."

Alex broke their silence.

"This town has everything, great mooring, shops, local 'catch of the day' and perfect location for a business right between Southampton and Bournemouth with easy access to the Isle of Wight. I think I would like to come back here one day and perhaps run a tour boat up and down this beautiful coast; wouldn't that be something?"

"It sure would be. That really would be something to work towards and who knows I might even retire down here and give you a hand, maybe put some money in to help get the business off the ground."

"I'll take you up on that, you mark my words."

The youth had a very definite gleam in his eye.

****

Back in London, they both took care of their day to day business until the phone call came.

Arriving just after the baby was born; they peered through the glass window at Amy holding her newborn.

Bob urged Alex forward.

"You'd better go in alone for a few minutes."

Amy held the baby out to him. He buried his face in the warm little body and cried. He cried for the blessing that Amy was all right, for the miracle of birth that he held in his arms and for the impending loss of his daughter, this tiny creature. Leaning over, he kissed Amy's cheek tenderly.

"Dear Amy, forgive me. I'll always love you, my sweet princess."

And both cried for the loss of their youth and the sheer joy of the tiny infant they held in their arms.

The three remained swaddled together for a few moments of supreme harmony and completeness, the baby softly gurgling and cooing between them.

Bob came in for a brief visit and admired the infant, a lovely baby girl with sunbeams running through her blond hair. Her eyes appeared to be blue grey but it was difficult to say at this early stage.

The day of Amy's discharge came all too quickly. Paperwork was subsequently signed and the baby Fiona christened and formally handed over to Amy's mother. Alex and Bob were returning to London but they were worried about Amy, she seemed reluctant to go with them, hardly speaking and withdrawn into herself. An extension was granted in the nursing home and it was agreed that she would rest up for another week or so before returning to London.

Harry had laid up his tug for repair and Alex took the opportunity to take a brief trip down to Southampton a couple of weeks later to see if he could persuade Amy to come back with him. Bob generously agreed to put her up until she got re-established. Sylvia was in favour of the proposition when it was put to her as it seemed the best thing for the girl; she needed to get on with her life.

Upon arrival in Southampton, Alex was shocked at the state of Amy, in his short absence she seemed to have wasted away and was being treated for anxiety and depression. He was really surprised when she actually agreed to go back to London with him.

They settled her in the little room, leaving her to organise herself but both were privy to her cries echoing through the wall.

"You'd better go and sit with her a while lad and quieten her down. We can't have this, it's too depressing."

Bob was getting increasingly fretful and fidgeting in his chair.

Alex sat with her for several nights until the early hours of the morning, and she wept for her loss and the way things had been. Long racking sobs flowed from deep within her rattling around his brain until he thought he couldn't bear another minute of it, and he held her remembering his mother crying for his father in the night so long ago.

Suddenly it stopped; she was ready to go to work. They relocated her to Frank's bakery where she worked assiduously learning the business and for a while appeared to be getting on top of her emotional turmoil, although she relied heavily on the doctor's prescriptions. She remained aloof from Alex and apart from that, everybody's routine returned to a reasonable level of norm until that fateful day.

****

The old man hung onto her frail body while they waited for the taxi. Frank was slipping away and Amy had known for some time that she was losing her dear friend. They didn't have long to wait for the taxi which dropped them at the hospital; immediately medical people were running here there and everywhere whisking him away from her. Dazed and confused, she at least had the presence of mind to go and get Bob and Alex. Upon arrival in Camden Town, she instinctively flew into Alex's arms forgetting their ongoing issues.

Bob came rushing towards them.

"What's going on, what's happened?"

"It's Frank," she gasped. "I got him to the hospital but he's not going to make it, I'm sure. You had better come back with me quick if you want to see him."

Sitting grimly round his bed, they all held their breath when Frank suddenly rallied smiling his usual good natured smile at all of them.

"Now what's all the fuss about? I'm as right as nine pence, just had a funny turn that's all."

He passed in and out of consciousness through the night and slipped away peacefully in the early hours. His younger sister appeared shortly afterwards, letting them know in very definite terms that she would take things from there; handle all the financial affairs, etc.

It was a sad threesome that made their way to Frank's bakery that day for the last time so that Amy could get her belongings out. They were silent, consumed with sorrow, each remembering their friend in their own way.

****

Bob set Amy up in the little room at the back of his home. The room was tiny but met all her needs and she had the privacy to come and go as she wished but still she remained distant. As soon as they arrived, she went quietly to the little room and filled with sadness, opened an envelope from Frank with a little note inside and a rhyme:

Bright and shiny button that you are,
Sending the blues on journey far
Making each day seem more worthwhile,
The kindness in your heart shown in your smile.
Such youth and such caring mirrored in your face,
Young people like you make the world a better place.
By your example a lesson is learned with others to share
Of humility, compassion and never ending care. ©

'Forgot where I found this little rhyme but I kept it and it must surely have been written just for you. You've been a lovely young friend to me, bringing warmth and brightness each and every day and I want you to have this little gift. Put it in your savings account and look after yourself, princess.'

Amy gasped at the generosity of Frank's cheque but still her grief was boundless and emptiness overtook her.

Sitting in the lounge trying to make small talk, Alex and Bob were striving to mute the sounds of her crying; she was unreachable by either of them so they left her to ride it out.

The next day saw her a little more composed but refusing to eat anything.

"Frank left me my wages and was also very generous to me. He must have known what was coming. I am going down the road to deposit it along with the last salary as I haven't had time to deal with it. I'll be back later."

Distancing herself, she stayed for a few weeks. One day Alex came home to find Bob waiting for him at the door.

"She's gone lad, said she had another job and accommodation, said she'll be in touch."

Bob handed him a note which he had found on the kitchen table.

'Dear Alex, forgive me but I can't do this anymore. I need to be away from you to sort myself out. I can't carry on with you as if nothing happened because it did. Don't try to find me; we both need a fresh start.'

Alex sat down at the table head in hands. His friend laid his hand on his shoulder.

"I'm here for you lad. If you need anything, just say the word."

The boy was disconsolate and giving him some privacy, Bob left him to the total abandonment of himself to grief.

Alex had known before even reading the note that she was lost to him.

Chapter 10
Life Back in London

When Alex moved in with Bob permanently, he converted the loft into nautical style accommodation. The rooms were in keeping with his work and lifestyle, and he was really happy with the result. Bob offered endless encouragement, as his mentor and confidant always caring and ready to listen; Alex loved sharing the same house with him.

They were sitting in quiet companionship in Bob's little sitting room which, although not fancy, was built for comfort. A chubby little velvet sofa having seen better times sat on a faded carpet, accompanied by a huge winged chair, pouffe and T.V., all of which made up the main features of the room. Bob was not much of a reader but there was a bookcase built into an alcove with a few books scattered randomly on the shelves and another chair in close proximity which he was occupying. Sitting forward he looked keenly at Alex.

"So how's it going on the tugs then?"

Since Harry had taken Alex permanently on payroll as a trainee, the youth had been totally involved determined to learn everything. Although he was only sixteen years old, because he had worked unofficially with Harry the previous year and had basic sea going experience, he was eligible to begin his apprenticeship.

"Absolutely fabulous, I'm just loving it. Harry's the best. It's going to take me a few years but I want to become a Master of Towing like Harry. After I've done a year or so working and learning deck duties, I'll be an Apprentice Mate. I'll have to work at the position for approximately four years and then I'll be a Mate of Towing, so after at least five years in all, I can qualify as Master of Towing, the pièce de résistance. Of course I'll have to take exams for each course section as I go along and I get to travel with Harry the length of the Thames to the estuary and offshore sometimes while I'm learning and get this, I'll be a skipper eventually, Bob, imagine that. I'll actually be in charge of my own boat."

"I'm so proud of you me boy, what a special little lad you are, you're a clever one, that's for sure."

Bob was completely overwhelmed by this time and groping around in his pocket for his handkerchief.

Alex leapt up and gave his friend a hug.

"And it's all because of you. You've given me a life and helped Amy and I'll not let you down ever again," he added emphatically.

"I'll take courses and exams all my life if I have to. You've given me a chance that I never would have had. I've already made a real mess of things and ruined Amy but I'll never give up trying to get her back and I swore to her mum that I'd send money for the baby every month for her trust fund and then like me she'll have a chance to better herself when she grows up."

By this time Bob was using his sleeve as he fumbled his way to the kitchen having given up on trying to find his hankie in his pocket.

Amy was gone and Alex was having a hard time dealing with it. Bad enough that Frank had passed away and now he'd lost Amy. It was the bitter end although he still had Sid and Elsie who were plugging away in the bakery as homely and comforting as always and good old Bob, his mentor and friend. What a blessing they were still in his life. Bob had been like a very young father to him, always ready to guide him and teach him not only focussing on the clandestine side of life.

****

Alex hadn't seen Fred for some time as he had been so busy and was no longer involved in the 'assignments' for Bob. *I must get to see Fred soon*, he thought.

When he got back to the shop later, he caught up with Bob.

"Bob, how's old Fred doing, haven't seen him in ages? Do you want to meet up with him in the café for a while to catch up on old times?"

"That would be great. I'll get in touch with him."

Bob was very obviously preoccupied with his latest acquisition. Since the late 1950s Britain had been booming with the arrival of TVs, dishwashers, washing machines and other labour saving devices designed for the home. Many homes were being equipped in keeping with the 'new age'. Even food had been more plentiful with the extradition of the food ration books and there was definitely more interest in the kitchen. Bob had been systematically embracing the 'mod con' era, and had acquired a TV and washing machine and was lovingly admiring his new dishwasher when Alex burst in.

"Well lad, what do you think of this beauty? After dinner we'll try it out. Don't worry about using too many plates and stuff, this little baby is going to solve all our problems. No more bribing matches to get out of washing the dishes. We simply rinse and dump in there. Isn't it great?"

Alex was impressed and the two spent the next half an hour pouring over the information book.

"OK, let's get this show on the road. The sooner we get dinner done, the sooner we can get our beer, pull up a couple of chairs and watch this magic machine take care of all our needs."

Which is exactly what they did.

****

Old Fred seemed much the same when they met up with him and made a great production of showing them his new wheelchair with all the latest bells and whistles. Post war years had seen a gradual change of view regarding the plight of disabled people. It had taken time but different forms of medical aids and assistance had become available to the handicapped through the National Health Service. The 1960s brought wheelchairs with optional power packs which were proving problematic, requiring modification and refinement. Fred had no interest in a motor of any sort and was thrilled to bits with his chair which had the added advantage of keeping his upper torso fit because he had to wheel it himself; always protecting his hands with heavy hide gloves. His life had taken on a whole different meaning for the better.

The little café to which Fred had first taken Alex was still there and the food consistently great. While prices were higher, they were certainly still very reasonable when compared with other restaurants which also lacked the personal service and the usual royal welcome from George.

"How you doing then old friend?" Bob shook Fred's outstretched hand as did Alex.

"The old legs bothering me a bit these days."

Fred looked dismal; his two friends howled with laughter once the penny had dropped and they'd thought about what he'd said. Old Fred hadn't lost his sense of humour in spite of the evil blow that had been dealt to him.

"Oh! For God's sake, cut it out," Bob said, slapping Fred on the arm. "Now let's order our food, I see that the menu is just as varied as it always was, lots of choice."

It was a great gathering for all three and they agreed unanimously not to leave it so long next time.

****

Alex's practical apprenticeship on the tugs and his studies filled his life now, particularly as he was gaining more and more certification and well on his path towards his goal as a skipper of his own vessel. It had taken him longer than he had expected but that was his choice. As a perfectionist, he agonised over every upcoming exam determined to score high marks and allowed himself extra study time to make sure he got it right and passed each time he was tested. In fact he figured if he stayed with it, he should qualify in about a year. Fortunately with all his studying, there was little time for brooding over his losses but he found time to keep up with the political scene and develop his keen interest in environmental sustainability.

Eventually the day arrived when Alex reached the coveted goal of Master of Towing, qualifying him to skipper his own vessel. What a day that was, Harry and Bob were hosting a celebratory party and Sid, Elsie, Dan and Rosalind were all joining the festivities. Sid, as usual, came through with the cake which Elsie had decorated with 'congratulations' and as many nonsensical folderols as she could possibly fit on top. Alex smiled when he saw it knowing the effort she put in for him and felt proud and so very grateful to have friends such as these gathered around him;

acknowledging that without their support and encouragement he may never have reached his goal.

****

Alex and Dan were thirty-four years old and had shared common interests throughout most of those years focussing specifically on issues such as self-improvement, political, environmental and nuclear disarmament. They and thousands of others had attended the huge public meeting held in London in 1958 officially launching Campaign for Nuclear Disarmament (CND). Both had avidly watched the progression of this seemingly hopeless fight in view of the ever increasing production of nuclear weapons. Nevertheless, their enthusiasm had not been daunted and the years not wasted in their further development, both remaining highly motivated and becoming extremely accomplished, well-educated and informed young men.

Dan had been instrumental in opening Alex's mind to the dilemma of the black immigrants, particularly as he was a staunch supporter and participant in the 1959 general election for the first African parliamentary candidate, David Pitt, in the north London constituency. Dan's work in the canvassing and campaigning for his idle was never ending and Alex also supported the cause with growing enthusiasm.

They were enjoying a coffee on one of their rare get-togethers and Dan's rambunctious enthusiasm was almost the cause of his being thrown out of the café as he was asked to lower his voice.

"Do you know Alex that David Pitt is a qualified doctor as well? He opened his own medical practice in Euston shortly after the war. He makes no distinction between black and white and always extends the same courtesy and compassion for everybody. He's given his life over to fighting for racial harmony on top of all his other attributes. The man's a walking miracle."

Dan had managed to get into a government position with the National Health Service and his commitment to better himself had proved an uphill battle, given the horrendous increase in violence and antagonism towards newcomers of his culture, coupled with the ever changing government agenda regarding immigration. Since British Citizenship had been granted to the colonies, the country was ill equipped to deal with the many thousands of newcomers to the island causing major governmental divide. Finally, in 1962 the inception of the *Commonwealth Immigrants Act* resulted in the restriction of non-white commonwealth immigrants from entering Britain without a government issued pass.

The Notting Hill Riot of several years later was so huge, it attracted media attention and racialism was rampant with major rumblings that the immigrants were taking all the employment, when in fact most of them were living below the poverty line in the worst areas of the country and renegaded to the lowest class of British culture. Following the riot, a major tear down of the run-down area of London took place in an effort to rejuvenate and infuse new life. It was a time of major political and social reform.

Alex and Dan had been part of the crowd in the subsequent 1968 Notting Hill carnival which was born to promote peace and miraculously it did, bringing about a lull in the animosity between the different cultural groups. Both men were remembering their first major family outing after the war in 1951 when, as young teens, they went to the Festival of Britain; that too was instigated to boost morale during the post-war years.

Part of the land-based festival had included a floating exhibition, the festival ship HMS Campania which had been fitted out and decorated as an extension of the main show stopping at towns along the coast, staying in each port for any time up to two weeks.

"Pity that the festival site was torn down later following a change in government and viewpoint," Dan pointed out, adding, "although it did make a good profit for the few months it ran and really gave Londoners a boost."

"Yes, it certainly did but isn't it ironical?" and Alex became very serious at this point, "That this same ship, following its service during the war should have been utilised as a festival ship to lift the spirits of a recovering race but instead the very next year it's re-fitted yet again, only this time to test an atom bomb off the Australian coast, potentially promoting more warfare. Talk about a dichotomy in ideals. You'd think there had been enough killing; sad too that the ship was scrapped a few years later."

"Yes it was and talking about bombs, what about the hydrogen bomb activated a few years after that off Christmas Island? It would seem there's no end to it, although hasn't it been great that there's been so much kicking and screaming in favour of nuclear disarmament? My God, the 50s were really something. We've certainly seen some changes over the years."

Alex agreed as Dan got launched yet again on another thoroughly stimulating topic.

"London is really moving forward now in its rebuilding. What do you think about The Barbican? It's that huge office development, apparently the biggest construction project ever in Europe. Built in 1969 with housing, a school, museum and art centre. It's so massive they reckon it won't be completed until 1975."

"No, I haven't seen it yet but I'm very impressed with the rebuilding programs generally and especially the movement to save the beautiful old Victorian houses. They've been demolishing them left right and centre because everybody thought they were ugly and the trend with the ones they have saved is to split them up into flats, restaurants and other business ventures, which I suppose is better than demolishing them altogether. The little terraces are quite attractive though, the message finally got through that these Victorians have a durability that the modern buildings lack and it's one way of dealing with the massive influx of people into the area."

Dan looked at his watch. "Oh hell, look at the time, we'd better break this up."

There was a mad scuffle to gather their knapsacks, etc. The friends hugged each other and shook hands.

"Until the next time Alex, stay in touch."

"Will do."

Another hug and the friends parted.

****

Alex sat by the river idly spinning stones across its surface, being an expert and always managing to get six or more jumps across its surface even on stormy days when the water was rough and angry.

How he had grown to love the Thames, knowing it with an intimacy to which few were privy, developing a deep understanding of all its moods and tantrums, likening its volatility to his own emotional state; up and down, up and down always craving the unobtainable, always pushing himself almost beyond endurance to achieve excellence either in work or play.

It was hard to imagine that the river had been officially declared dead, devoid of life but following the war and improvements to London's sewage system, life was returning of its own volition. Also, in these latter years, there had been much more environmental awareness regarding the use of pesticides and other toxics. Alex too nurtured his ever-growing interest and knowledge of natural history and evolution, and was pleased to see that tighter regulations were being put in place in an attempt to protect the environment.

Today the river played games with his senses, the air hummed with the sounds of a thousand birds competing with the humming of the rushing water making its way to the North Sea. In the city centre, the Thames was incarcerated by its borders of concrete but further out of town it harboured a multitude of wildlife on its lush banks, all grappling for space amongst the reeds and grasses. He smiled as he watched the antics of a river vole and marvelled at the plumage of the kingfisher, which had even managed to adapt and become resilient to city life and human abominations inflicted on nature. He'd been fascinated to see them nesting in concrete and pipes in and around the Thames; their beauty contrasting sharply with the man-made ugliness of the confines of the river.

A great crested grebe adorned in his exotic cloak strutted around; his gait ridiculous with legs being set too far back on his body and definitely not designed for walking. He was not to be put off; however and was magnificent as he flaunted his good looks while he still had them, probably knowing that come winter his attire would be renegaded back to drab winter garb.

The wind began to pick up; the river appearing to flow faster than the educated guess of eight miles per hour. His mood echoed the change and again the restless that always plagued him returned with a vengeance. He thought again of the last time he had seen Amy, how exquisitely beautiful she was. He likened her to a fairy princess he had seen adorning an exclusive Christmas arrangement in one of the classy London stores, when he was a boy. He had stared in awe through the window at the vision of loveliness. When was he going to accept that not only was she lost to him but their daughter as well? He indulged himself in a moment of fantasy dreaming of a life they could have had, which they had lived for such a short time and then lost.

The stones were hitting the water with growing ferocity and all-consuming regret engulfed him.

"God, I'm drowning. I've got to make changes, get away from here get my head straight. I've been on the tugs up and down the Thames for twenty odd years and yep it's time for change, I'll take up the option of the job in the West Country."

His voice was hoarse, he was shouting but there was no one to hear; his eyes burned with emergent tears but there was no one to see and as he stumbled up the narrow overgrown path, his beloved river laughed merrily in his wake.

Chapter 11
The West Country

The flat was perfect; exactly what Alex had been looking for and more with two bedrooms, two bathrooms, spacious kitchen with good dining annex and to top it off, a study with a great balcony leading off to the most spectacular view of the ocean. St. Ives had been his favoured location and to have found such a gem was astounding. The owners had asked him if he would consider a short-term rental and mentioned that they would be selling in the near future. Alex had been looking for an investment property and everything about this accommodation fitted the bill. He would have no trouble renting it out or using it as a vacation spot himself if he left the west coast. He knew Bob would just love it as well.

"I think it would work to our mutual advantage if you'd allow me the first offer," he had conferred to the owners. "A lot more lucrative don't you think without any of the extraneous costs in fees and such? The place is a good fit for my needs." He didn't want to appear too effusive about the prospect as he felt it might reflect on their offering price.

Alex had not wasted his time over the years and was now at the top of his field on the tugs. Having lived frugally, he had managed to save a substantial sum. The owners had obviously reflected on the savings involved with a private sale arrangement and his opportunity to purchase came sooner than he expected; a mere two months after the commencement of his tenancy and furthermore, his offer was accepted with no quibbling. He was ecstatic. He knew a good investment when he saw one and this was certainly one.

Located in one of the most desirable tourist areas, St. Ives was a picturesque port offering a safe, sheltered harbour although its wreck history was long standing. Many vessels attempting the western approach had been claimed by treacherous seas over the years; nevertheless, the small boating community boasted immense charm and beauty guaranteeing the tourist a fabulous stay in the West Country. Cobbled streets bordered by quaint stone dwellings and businesses packed in wall to wall constituted a regular cornucopia of delights for everybody. The area had always been known as a popular drinking venue being littered with dozens of charming little pubs steeped in history, the most prominent being over 700 years old. Alex was very interested in art and had promised himself visits to the arts club unchanged in 100 years and the museum remodelled from the original home and studio of one of the local artists. The entire area was an artist's dream with its light reflecting qualities; attracting them from all over the world and introducing art colonies to the area. Yes, he had definitely made a wise judgement call in coming to this awe-inspiring place.

****

Alex's decision to leave London and the Thames had also been influenced by the regressing commercial tug and barge industry due to the inception of container traffic, triggering a decline in the dockyards. He was very well positioned to take up his new employment and make the easy transition to operating the different types of tugs, as he had always been big on updating his skills in keeping with economical and technical changes in the industry. Over the years, he had demonstrated excellent crew management abilities specifically in safety management systems on each of the vessels for which he was responsible. Safety practice was a given and second nature to his crew members. He never allowed inexperienced personnel to be exposed to high risk situations without extensive training and constant supervision, which was meticulously logged and included lifesaving and firefighting.

His new employer had snapped him up and Alex was thrilled to take on new challenges and be involved in many diverse marine roles such as search and recovery, obstruction and waste removal and a new venture for him, that of commercial diving projects, the latter of particular interest in the event of him ever running his own tour boat. Diving equipment would be a prerequisite on any cruiser he owned in the future, he had already decided. The position he had accepted would encompass the general radius of the Land's End Peninsula, a treacherous coastline to which the adventurous Alex was drawn like the moth to the flame.

****

What a great bunch his new crew members were. They gave him not only a royal welcome the first time he boarded the vessel for his introductory tour but also insisted on holding a bash on the wharf in one of the more ancient pubs as an official welcome to the team.

Grabbing a paper on his way down the wharf, he had made a point of getting there early so that he could relax before any of the group arrived and was enjoying a glass of the local Cornish ale when an article on David Pitt caught his eye in the newspaper. The politician had been accepted that year into the House of Lords upon the recommendation of the Labour Party leader Harold Wilson, history in the making. This was the beginning of non-whites in parliament. *Have to give Dan a call later*, he thought, *of course he obviously would know about this as well*. Glancing up from the paper, he was fascinated by the pub and surroundings and could almost picture smugglers of hundreds of years ago making their way stealthily up the wharf with whatever spoils they could haul up the steep incline. Usually their treasures would be hidden in caves up and down the Cornish coast for pick up when the conditions allowed.

The day was perfect with the sea casting its cerulean waters softly up and down the picturesque bay. Jack hailed him from the doorway. He was herding the rest of Alex's work colleagues ahead and they were in high spirits laughing and joking. Alex had taken to Jack immediately on their first meeting. He was a quiet, easy going man, one of those solid individuals who, once your friend, always your friend. Very soon the room was filled with their comradery. Appetites finally appeased, they all raised their glasses and toasted Alex, welcoming him once again to the team. Later they wrapped up the splendiferous evening with a dart tournament, which Jack and Alex's team won hands down. Permanent teams were established that night and this sport was to be their favourite recreation. Each player took the game very seriously looking forward with huge enthusiasm to their next 'play off'.

One evening after their shift was finished, Jack slapped Alex on the back.

"When are you coming home to meet the family then, Judy keeps asking me? She wondered if you are free on

Saturday night about 7:00 and would like to come for dinner."

"Yes, I would and thanks for asking me I would really like that." Alex emphasised. "What kind of wine does Judy like?"

"Oh any sweet white, she's not well up on the names or years for that matter. There are some really good local wines, I don't think you can go wrong with any of them if you really want to pick one up, although it really isn't necessary, you're our guest."

"Well, I would like to and thanks again for the invite."

The following Saturday saw Alex grasping a bunch of flowers and wine being greeted by the loveliest Cornish woman one could imagine. She was everything he expected, hugging him warmly in welcome and urging him into the little stone cottage filled with the wonderful aroma of home cooking. His mouth was watering even before he sat down. Hand in hand, two little children came into the room and their mother introduced them.

Walking away that night, Alex felt envy for the first time in his life. He had always been a firm believer in getting what he wanted for himself but he had messed up and his heart cried out for what Jack had in his loving little family.

****

Alex had been with his company for a year only and knew it was really a bit early to be thinking of taking a break back in London but Dan was getting married to Rosalind. He was to be best man, an occasion that he couldn't miss as Dan had been and still was his lifelong friend. Alex had offered the couple his flat for a few days after the wedding and they were over the moon about it, particularly when they saw the photos and what the area had to offer for a perfect vacation and honeymoon.

He was staying with Bob for his short visit and it was just as if he'd never left. Both settled right back into the same routine as when they shared accommodation previously. It was Alex's first morning and they were enjoying one of their two-hour brunches.

"By the way Bob, how's old Fred doing? You haven't mentioned him yet."

He saw Bob's face cloud over.

"Poor old Fred's gone. I didn't want to mention it as you've just got here and it was only a couple of weeks ago."

There were a few moments of silence as both men contemplated the situation.

"Well, he had a good run given all the physical problems and he never let it get him down, always happy it seemed. What happened?"

"The doc reckoned he had a brain aneurysm, it was very quick."

"He was one of the best was old Fred."

Alex was still trying to get used to the idea.

"Bob," he was looking very serious and Bob could see the question he'd been skirting around was imminent.

"So have you seen Amy?"

"Well, she has been working at Sid's place since you went to the West Country. She's a huge asset to him because she knows the business having spent so much time with Frank. She's very private now, Alex, not half as gregarious as she used to be, very quiet and keeps herself to herself. Sid is just glad she's helping him out."

"Does she know I'm back in the city for a bit?"

"Well, I did mention you were coming home to Sid and Elsie and, by the way, they're really looking forward to seeing you and catching up on all your news. So yes, in answer to your question, I'd say there's a good chance one or the other told her about your visit. Alex, I'd let sleeping dogs lie if I were you. It's been a long time and it looks like Amy has decided to go it alone. She doesn't encourage anybody around her now. She's not the same person. Sid hasn't ever seen a man friend or any friends for that matter. I think after all this time if she was going to make her move towards you she would have done so by now. I'm sorry to be so blunt lad but I've watched you wear your heart on your sleeve long enough and it's time you got on with your life, apart from killing yourself with work."

"I appreciate your concern Bob but…"

"Yeah, yeah," Bob interrupted, cutting him off in mid-ships, "shooting my mouth off again so I'll just put a sock in it. Now about this wedding day after tomorrow, what the dickens am I going to wear?"

Alex was relieved that there was a change of pace and harmony was restored.

"Let's clear the crocks away, go out and do a bit of shopping. I'm in trouble in that department myself. I think we both need a makeover."

"Oh and by the way Alex, Sid and Elsie are going to the wedding."

Bob made a quick exit up the stairs before Alex could ask the other obvious question and that subject was closed as far as he was concerned.

That evening they returned more than happy with their new wardrobe acquisitions, which, while formal, were very adaptable suits of fine quality and could be worn at other festive gatherings. Both considered themselves in good shape for the celebrations.

Alex hurried to the church the next morning for the dress rehearsal with Dan and Rosalind, after which Dan took him to one side and told him that Amy would also be attending the ceremony.

"I knew it would be difficult for you Alex but we've all been friends for so long that she had to be included, particularly as she is working with Sid and Elsie at the moment and they are attending as well. It would have been shabby not to have issued the invitation."

"Everything's cool friend, I absolutely agree and I actually expected she'd be there."

Alex spoke speciously, keeping his voice even, hoping he sounded calm and collected about the whole situation.

That afternoon he took a walk through the old haunts to try and get his mind off the thought of seeing Amy again. How would he handle it? He wondered. Well, handle it, he would. There would be no dramatics; he would be polite and approachable.

Wandering through Primrose Hill, he could see that it was now an upper class area, obviously very expensive. The Victorian properties, now back in favour, were in great demand and beautifully restored to their original grandeur with elaborate cornicing and extensively embellished exteriors, becoming a major influence on prices in the area.

****

The day of the wedding dawned and a major panic ensued for Alex and Bob who were late getting out of their beds as usual. The wedding couple were perfect for each other it seemed, both radiant with happiness, positively glowing as they went through their vows which they had authored themselves for this their special day.

At first he didn't spot her, then in unison, their eyes met. Alex thought his heart would stop. He wondered if the palpitations in his neck were visible. The erratic throbbing had always been a problem plaguing him every time he was in a stressful situation. He reckoned it was a throwback to his childhood. Locked and bound together in their ephemeral world, both were oblivious to the soft droning of the ceremony in the background, then bodies were pushing him forward to complete his duties as best man.

The moment passed as all moments do. He was shaken. His feelings for her had not diminished over the years, if anything were stronger. The pain in his chest was unimaginable as he went through the motions, completing requirements for the ceremony.

She was nowhere to be seen in the reception room later. In desolation, he moved into the garden area to clear his mind and there she was before him, abounding with a beauty that was hers alone. Unaware of his presence being lost in her own world, his step on the gravel caught her off guard. Their attempt at conversation was unsuccessful being stilted and polite, although she did seem interested in his work and such but very obviously steered clear of any personal connotations.

Forfeiting his well-laid resolutions, Alex jumped head in.

"Amy, what are we doing? Is there any chance for us? I love you; I always have and always will."

"Alex, there is no us, not anymore."

The touch of asperity in her voice was unfamiliar to him, her finality sending chills through his body.

"We both have our own lives now and you are no longer a part of mine. That's the way it has to be. We had our chance and lost it when we threw it to the wind so carelessly without a thought for the future or the consequences of our actions."

"Amy please…" but she was walking away from him.

"Alex don't, please don't."

Then she was gone, past the group of guests, out of the main exit and out of his life yet again.

****

Alex, hardly aware of Bob's voice, grabbed the drink that was pushed in his trembling hand and knocked it back with a vengeance. He continued to drink throughout the rest of the reception until Bob urged him forward towards the exit, stopping briefly to extend their salutations and wish Dan and Rosalind a wonderful honeymoon in the West Country. Upon arrival at Bob's, they both slurped their way through the rest of the night, Bob knowing that under the riotous frivolity, he had a friend whose heart was fragmenting into a thousand pieces.

The next morning brought Alex a hangover from hell while his friend fed him the foulest tasting concoctions he'd ever experienced and with each gulp prayed he never would again. The one saving grace was that Bob managed to keep his witticisms to himself.

****

Back on the west coast he threw himself into his work and as if that wasn't enough for him, he volunteered for the lifeboat rescue services. He would be working in coordination with rescue operations in Padstow and St. Agnes to the east and Sennen Cove to the west. His life was now fully booked, leaving absolutely no time for dwelling on past matters and that was just the way he wanted it.

****

Jovial as always, Jack came to pick up his friend. They were going out on Jack's fishing boat and had not been out long when the weather took a turn for the worst, a sudden squall coming up, a situation familiar to the area. Seeing the massive wall of water rolling ferociously towards them, they knew all too well they were done for. Capsized in seconds, they found themselves clinging to whatever boat contents were floating. They hung for what seemed hours; singing songs, cracking jokes, anything to stay in touch with each other and keep their thoughts away from how bitterly cold they were. Alex could see his friend was failing fast.

"Hang on Jack; for God's sake hang on, just a bit longer. They'll be coming for us soon."

He closed his eyes and when he opened them Jack was gone, then he saw the lights.

"Too late, too bloody late," he screamed wondering if he should just let go of the debris he clung to and stop fighting. Darkness was closing in. Waves engulfing him, freezing cold, he was slipping, slipping, then there were lights, more lights, suddenly warmth spreading throughout his body, then slipping again but now into a warm world; voices, was that the sound of angels? Jack are you there?

The nurse was leaning over him shaking him gently.

"Take a deep breath, just breath."

He was in hospital. They told him he had been there for some days. Realisation hit him, how was he going to look Judy in the face? He was alive and her husband lost to her. Surely she would ask why he was saved and not her Jack, a question he was asking himself.

****

As soon as he was out of hospital, he made the visit he had been dreading. Looking into their faces, the children with a glimmer of hope but acceptance written on Judy's, he averted his gaze.

"Alex, it's okay, don't fret yourself."

She didn't cry, like all the other wives whose daily torment had come to fruition. They were brave stalwart women who shed their tears in private, knowing they were never to see their men again.

Jack's body was recovered a couple of days later. After the accepted period, his ashes cast from the Roseland Peninsula as was his wish. He had been born very close to the beautiful church, St. Just in Roseland where his roots were. Alex had listened many times when his friend had told him about the thirteenth century church and vowed he would visit in the next few days and honour Jack's memory.

It was all Jack had said it would be. The walk through the little church yard had been a cathartic experience, ridding his mind of torment, gently guiding him into another world of supreme serenity. The little stone church was surrounded by varying aspects of openness to the water and multiple paths bordered by rocks leading to the quietude and shelter of magnificent trees and shrubs. Pausing to look at the ancient headstones in the little cemetery, a soft breeze caressing his face, Alex was thinking of the evanescence of life, so precious, so brief, in direct contrast to death's permanence with its promise of a life hereafter.

****

He made out the bank draft to Mrs. Sarah Rowlings, in Trust for Fionna Rowlings. Alex was making his final official contribution for his daughter`s needs and education; a contribution which he had made for the last twenty odd years regardless of where he was situated. He sat back in his chair, his coffee now cold on the desk. Rain beat steadily on the window pane as he looked out over a choppy sea. His daughter had qualified as a registered nurse and had plans for further education in order to specialise in one of the many medical areas which were of interest to her. He felt proud, and humble that he had been allowed to participate to some degree in her success. The daughter he had never known had obviously turned out well and was entering an honourable profession.

Amy was never far from his thoughts and when he closed his eyes in sleep, she invaded his dreams with her pure sweetness. He wondered if she ever thought of him, he doubted it. She had left him under no delusions the last time they had met. She had said he was no longer a part of her world; well she was his world and even though he was leaving their homeland for another country, he was resigned to the fact that she would be part of him in his new world and into infinity.

****

The following few days were to be spent in London and then Alex was catching a flight to Canada; a country which had always intrigued him, to begin yet another chapter in his life. May as well do it while he was still young enough, he thought and with enough gumption to take the plunge. He had accepted a position as Mate on a tug boat and once again would be involved in hauling and rescue operations but also salvage and ice breaking, new ventures again. He would be taking up this option in one week. The company ran tugs out of Halifax, Nova Scotia and with yet another dangerous coast to conquer, Alex was looking forward to the challenge of new pastures, although he still yearned for the unreachable.

Chapter 12
Canada

Alex stopped at Bob's front door, fist bunched ready to cause his usual disturbance but the door was flung open beating him to the punch.

Bob appeared grinning broadly and practically pulled him across the threshold.

"Ha, got you that time, you're pipped at the post."

Bob had arranged a special evening for Alex and invited all their closest friends. The lounge was shrouded in darkness when Alex finally arrived. Hearing a muffled giggle in the back regions of the room, he snapped on the light and walked right into the surprise bash. Everyone descended upon him in one herd and shrieks of laughter reverberated off the walls.

"Late as usual," Dan bellowed.

"What have you been doing?"

"I had a last look at the old hangouts and said goodbye to a couple of people. Not much really although must say I felt a bit nostalgic."

"Well, you'll be back again, you mark my words. You've got the old country in your bones, it's imbedded in you. We'll all be seeing you again pretty soon, I reckon. It's one thing to go down to the West Country, it's quite another to leave your homeland, your roots."

Harry's voice was tremulous. He had grown to love Alex just as Bob did. Whenever the pair of them looked at him, each had a vision of a freckle-faced youth staring back at them. A determined youth both had come to realise, with an unbreakable tenacity to succeed. He was very much respected and held in high regard by all those who were close to him and recognised his strength and forthrightness. Those people, hand-picked by Bob, were all present on that special evening.

As always, it was a grand party. Bob, a true raconteur, held the floor. A number of the attendees got up and either roasted Alex or enlightened their audience on his good points or failings but Bob was right in there, putting up a good show having all the party goers in stitches as he ribbed Alex unceasingly, although privately he was devastated at losing his protégé and having a hard time accepting Alex's decision to leave his friends and loved ones.

Everybody else also felt at a loss because Alex was leaving the country for an indeterminate time but they all made merry, making the best of the situation and of course extended their best wishes. There were a few tears shed; however, when at the close of the festivities, each stepped forward to wish him a fond farewell with hopes to see him back again soon. All, without exception, were wondering when he was going to stop trying to outrun his past.

****

The flight to Canada was long and hard. All passengers were obliged to wear their seatbelts most of the way, an annoyance but necessary because of the foul weather and turbulent conditions. There was a short stopover in Moncton, New Brunswick and then on to Halifax, Nova Scotia. A little excitement for everybody ensued when, upon descent, a small plane flew into the flight path, forcing the pilot to circle the airport to attempt another approach.

Upon alighting from the plane, freezing cold ripped Alex's breath right out of his body sending him into uncontrollable spasms of coughing.

"Why in God's name did I pick this time of year?"

He was muttering and didn't care if he was overheard by the other passengers filing along beside him.

"Talk about masochistic, must have been out of my mind."

He had been so eager to make a complete break that he hadn't taken the weather situation into consideration and had made his preparations as soon as his governmental entry papers to Canada had arrived.

Alex had taken a hotel room adjacent to the airport for convenience until he got his bearings. The accommodation was sparsely furnished but adequate for his needs. Being too exhausted to eat, he took a really hot shower, which helped, as he thought his bones had crystalised with the cold and that he would never warm up again. Crawling gratefully into bed, he fell into an unconscious stupor in seconds.

The next morning, he selected his warmest clothes and was greeted enthusiastically as he positioned himself comfortably in the little dining room.

"How you doing then, eh?"

Since stepping off the plane in the Maritimes, he had noticed everybody was very friendly and outgoing, most of them finishing their sentences with 'eh'. The cook-cum-waiter was no exception.

His breakfast was plain but wholesome and plenty of it, cereal and toast with actual marmalade which delighted him as marmalade was not, it seemed, readily available in many eateries and a pot of good strong tea was also included.

Reclining back in his chair later letting his food settle, he was hailed once again from the back regions.

"So how was it then, eh?"

He smiled in spite of himself.

"It was terrific, thanks very much. Any chance of getting a taxi to the docks in about half an hour, I have to meet somebody?"

Alex wanted to leave himself plenty of time; he was meeting the tug company owner and wanted to make sure there were no hitches.

That settled, he made his way back to his room, brushed his teeth, packed the rest of his bag and moved briskly downstairs to settle up his bill.

"Was it a good stay, then, eh?"

This time from the desk clerk.

Well, it looks like they're all at it, Alex thought.

The taxi dropped him in front of the company offices and John Maclaren, Alex's new boss, held out his hand in greeting.

"Welcome to Canada and Halifax. How was your flight? I was wondering how you'd be coping with the weather, we've been getting it pretty bad this last week."

Alex immediately noticed the 'eh' was missing.

'It could have been worse, I suppose, it's just the cold, it'll take a bit of getting used to."

You haven't seen anything yet, believe me."

"Well, I don't know anything about that, all I know is that it's what we in England call brass monkey weather, cold enough to freeze the…"

Laughing a deep full-bellied laugh, John finished the quote for Alex.

"We speak the same language here, you know, for the most part. Most of the European extractions here were originally Brits and the rest Irish, Scottish, all from the Islands. We have our own First Nations people, the Mi'kmaq who were here long before any of us and our black community who first set foot on our shores in the early 1600s. So you can see, we're just a mixed bunch of apostates that's what we are, also known as Newfies in Newfoundland. You'll be quite at home here."

Alex was already warming to him and things were getting off to a good start.

He had researched and secured accommodation for rent in Halifax before he left England and was well pleased when he saw it following his meeting. It was a small self-contained annex off one of the big old traditional houses bordering the inlet in Halifax. The 1960s and on had seen the area in and around the harbour designated 'historic' and gradually restored. Alex favoured the old heritage architectural styles and saw some resemblance to areas in and around London and the west coast of England. Once again he was privy to a water view from his flat; this time of the harbour; which naturally was different to the little inlet of St. Ives but nonetheless beautiful and as he was to find out, exquisite at sunset and sunrise.

His work was going to be varied covering three areas, that of typical harbour tug boat work, some handling of commodities such as forest products and the major part of his duties, of most interest to Alex, the towing of offshore drilling platforms for the oil and gas industry, and marine salvage work. During winter months, he could be called upon to assist in ice breaking operations, another entirely new venture for him and he was eager to get started.

Alex settled into his new routine quickly and efficiently. He was really taken with his colleagues noting the character similarities of all seafaring crew members. Their lives threatened almost daily with treacherous conditions and the decisions they were forced to make in the face of extreme danger, made them a unique group. They hung together in the tacit knowledge that their team members could be called upon to save their very lives at any given time; a daunting prospect. On the other hand when they played, they played hard, loving their get-togethers with their mates in the local pubs, with jokes flying around for hours and some pretty hard drinking on occasion by way of relief.

****

That winter was something the like of which Alex had never experienced in his life with temperatures well below freezing, lasting all day through January to April and the ever lurking mist and fog conditions allowing little of the feeble sun through the haze. It really took some getting used to. The old balaclava took on a whole new meaning for Alex. It covered his entire face except his eyes and mouth, and he made sure never to be without it or his gloves in winter. The risk of frost bite was a very real thing as evidenced on some of his mates' faces and hands which were missing the odd chunk of flesh here and there, where their owners had been careless about protecting themselves properly. Nevertheless, few work days were missed because of wretched weather conditions but danger was always present whenever the boat went out. The grim reaper of the ocean waited albeit impatiently for his next victims.

Summers were pleasantly warm, however, with his first finally arriving. Alex met it headlong with joy, not realising how much the weather affected him and his moods. He took a trip up to Citadel Hill, a historic site and military fortress established in 1935. Fortunately, its value had been recognised before it was demolished and a gradual restoration program was put in place beginning in the late 1940s, restoring it to its original Victorian state. Housing the Halifax Army Museum, the Nova

Scotia Museum and the Maritime Museum of the Atlantic, the site became the most historical attraction in Atlantic Canada; a major tourist pull.

Alex was particularly fascinated by the statue of the giant Angus MacAskill who originated from Scotland and came to Canada as a child. He grew to be over 7-1/2 feet high weighing more than 400 pounds. He was, apparently, a natural giant in perfect health with no medical condition and his memorial statue was built overlooking Halifax. Standing beside this behemoth, Alex found himself to be severely lacking physically and determined to visit the little cemetery in Englishtown on Cape Breton Island, where the gentle giant had been laid to rest beside the graves of his mother and father following his death in 1863.

Following the daily noonday salute of the ceremonial gun, also used for 21 gun salutes, Alex enjoyed his picnic lunch at the summit and revelled in the warm sunshine and the magnificent view of the city and its huge harbour. It was one of those perfect days not to be forgotten, definitely one of his most fascinating in the Maritimes.

At the first opportunity, Alex visited Peggy's Cove, a tiny fishing village surrounded in folklore offering varying reasons for its name but one popular theory was that the cove had been named after a lone survivor from a shipwreck in the mid-1800s who subsequently took up residence there. The community had been built up since the 1800s following the governmental land grants issued to the first settlers of German descent who survived on fishing and farming where possible. Very basic facilities had been added over the years in the form of a cannery, store and school to name a few. Little wooden houses built on the rocks surrounded the cove and while appearing somewhat stark, possessed a character all of their own. Alex had picked a great day to visit the little cove with the sun glistening off boats of all shapes and sizes, used mainly for fishing. Clustered around the inlet, the vessels added to the charm of the little cove.

Being a seafaring man, Alex was particularly interested in the lighthouse which had perched precariously on its rock base at the point since the early 1900s. He made sure that he arrived early in the day so that he could experience the famous morning light radiating from the point first hand. What an awesome sight, although he didn't linger on the rocks for long being all too well aware of the dangers of sudden waves which had swept many a person away.

****

They were all in high spirits as they climbed into the car. Alex was going on a road trip to Charlottetown, Prince Edward Island with a couple of his crew member friends, Darren and Sean. Darren was visiting relatives in Charlottetown who ran a charming old hotel which boasted a fabulous lobster dinner and he had invited his mates along thinking it would be a fun trip. Although they only had time for two night stops, Alex was thrilled to be getting the chance to go with people who were familiar with the area and had promised to take him around and see what they could in the time. They figured they could get to the island in good order as all three were taking turns at the driving.

Their trip included a ferry crossing at Caribou saving them travel time. Although it was a short passage over the Northumberland Strait, the three did manage to inhale a tasty lunch of fish and chips and a round of beer while listening to live Maritime music by local artists, followed by a quick walk around the deck to look at the porpoises swimming alongside the ferry. Alex's first view of Charlottetown intrigued him, particularly its unusual shape caused by its situation between three converging rivers in the harbour. He had picked up some travel books on the area and was looking forward to some in-depth reading about the island and its history.

Upon arrival, they were greeted by Darren's uncle. Alex could see immediately where Darren got his raw sense of humour, it was pouring out of the older man's mouth, promising to be a riotous dinner gathering that night.

"Molly, are you there? Our visitors have arrived."

A smiling little woman appeared wiping floured hands on her apron.

"Nice to see you again Sean and pleased to meet you Alex."

He was surprised at the strength of her grip; *Must be all that flour rolling and humping meals backwards and forwards from the kitchen to the dining room*, he was thinking.

"Yes, you have to watch out for that grip," her husband said jovially, noting Alex wince. "You don't want to get on the wrong side of her, that's for sure."

"You watch your mouth; you'll be giving our visitors the wrong impression."

"Yes and feisty as well."

Darren's uncle made a hasty retreat before his wife could get another one in, grabbing a couple of bags and heading up the luxuriously carpeted stairs bordered by the colonial style bannisters.

"Are you coming then? I'll show you to your rooms."

Later, having freshened up, the three friends took themselves out to see the town and what a lovely historical town it was with so much to explore, Alex didn't know where to look first.

"As we have another day tomorrow, perhaps we could take a drive around the island a bit, wouldn't that be great?"

Sean and Darren agreed wholeheartedly.

Alex had picked up a floral arrangement while they were out and presented it to Molly with a flourish when they arrived back that evening. Beaming with pleasure, she had placed it in the centre of the table. They sat down that night to mouth-watering fare of the fresh lobster dinner that Alex had heard so much about and an enticing basket of home-made bread and soup for starters. When the coffee and liqueurs arrived, they were accompanied by wild apple crisp with Canadian maple cream. Boy oh boy, what a blow-out that was. Alex could hardly move when they finally got up from the table and headed for the lounge.

Their trip around part of the island the next day was everything that Alex could have hoped. Beautiful flat meadows accented by occasional softly rolling hills and a coastline that was breathtaking. Nova Scotia was known for the world's highest tides evidenced by the erosions on the cliffs and miles of superb beaches and caves to explore, with the more rocky peninsulas being broken up by numerous lighthouses on route. The three friends didn't get to see the whales, a common sight around the island but the day was another one to be brought out of the memory chest once in a while and remembered with joy.

Spirits were high when they all piled into the car the next day on their way to the ferry. It had been a well needed break which would set them up for what was to come.

****

Summer was over all too soon again and Alex had begun to shrink from the thought of another winter but it was on him once again. Since the trauma of losing Jack on the west coast of England, he had suffered odd bouts of severe depression, some lasting for days. His friend was pushing his way into Alex's thoughts more and more. In fact, every time he braved another storm off the Canadian east coast, Jack's smiling face was before him and once again he would relive the horror of that night and the last time he had looked into his friend's face before he sank beneath the waves.

It's an omen, he thought, *I've lost my edge, time to pack it in and stop putting my life on the line so casually. I'll head west to Vancouver maybe get into the tour boat business, run a cruiser off Vancouver and down the west coast. God knows, I've thought about it for so long I may as well do it while I still can.*

Once again reaching into his reservoir of tenacity and determination, Alex spent the next few months putting his plans in place. He researched every job opportunity focussing more on private cruising, as opposed to the heavy duty type of work he had been doing on the tugs. Once again he found he was heavily in demand because of his qualifications, receiving an exceptionally positive response to his enquiries and finally lined himself up with several potential job opportunities. Carefully selecting his choices from one to four, he contacted each with a view of setting up interviews. He was particularly interested in one tour boat owner who worked independently with his one cruiser, as opposed to one of the bigger tour boat companies operating fleets of vessels.

His phone conversation with Rick, the owner, was very encouraging and they hit it off right away. Rick was to be his first interview, followed on successive days by the other three, so he was in good shape he surmised for yet another major move. Finalising his plans, he sent up thanks once again to the powers that be that he had made it through another winter unscathed.

Chapter 13
Amy Goes Home

A member of the Salvation Army found her unconscious on the steps of their building and she was subsequently placed in one of the rehabilitation shelters. By some miracle, she had not succumbed to the hardcore drugs but years of anxiety disorders and anti-depression tablets, coupled with lack of proper nourishment had done her no good. Fortunately, she had sought help at the eleventh hour.

****

It was a bright sunny day. She sat by the window actually feeling good to be alive, enjoying the warmth of the sun penetrating her body as a soothing balm. They had been kind to her and nursed her back to health, and she was eternally grateful.

The manager of the establishment came in and sat down.

"Amy, your mother has been trying to find you. She wants you to go home."

"She wants me to go home, that can't be. There must be some mistake."

Her eyes were wide; her face strained trying to grasp what she had just heard.

"No, it's true. She got the Salvation Army to try to find you and I've just got off the phone with them. She wants you to come home and she left a message. *If you find her tell her I love her and I always have. Bill is dead. Please come home.*"

Amy was taking deep gasps of air and quiet sobs built in momentum, wracking her poor frame until it seemed she would fall apart. Her manager moved forward and laid her hand on the young woman's shoulder.

"Come, come, let's get a hold on ourselves. We have some decisions and plans to make. We're here to help, that's our job. Wipe your eyes now and we'll go and get a pot of tea and talk."

Blowing her nose vigorously, Amy was valiantly trying to get herself together. She stood up decisively.

"I'll go and get myself cleaned up, and I'll meet you in the lounge in half an hour if that's alright?"

Returning the warm smile directed at her, Amy left the manager and hurried towards the stairs turning and looking back over her shoulder as she reached the threshold. The reassuring nod of encouragement she received filled her with new resolve.

"I won't be long," she said as she hastened to the upper level and the sanctity of her room.

****

Walking up the path, she paused to take in the unchanged beauty of the garden. The air was aromatic, her senses absorbing all of the delicate perfumes, particularly the roses, their fragrance evoking memories of her past and childhood. The gorgeous Albertine rambling rose, now almost twenty feet, clambering up the back of the house, caught her full attention with its lovely salmon to pink flowers, the elite of ramblers. She had been astonished to discover it had been introduced in France in the early 1920s but had always seemed so British to her, probably because it was so popular and firmly entrenched in English gardens. A wonderful welcome for her homecoming; the blooms were just opening; hopefully she would be allowed to stay and enjoy the exquisite flowers through June and July. Further down the garden, the graceful laburnum was still showing the remains of its pendulous yellow blooms from late spring, as was the lilac, boasting varying shades of purple and then joy of joy the green, green grass reaching down to the sea beyond; instilling a sense of completeness and such peace suffusing the very soul. Am I really here? She kept asking herself. What a paradise, I don't ever want to leave this place again. Please God let me be allowed to stay.

Suddenly, there was her mother coming forward to meet her. There was a huge difference in her, the years had taken their toll; she looked so much older, although her smile was as warming and engaging as always. Her arms were outstretched in welcome to receive her daughter and they clung together. Finally her mother gently disengaged herself.

"Come let's sit in the arbour for a few minutes. This little place is my favourite spot, my 'magic' spot. It grounds me, gives me a base, a sense of being one with my soul while putting all the wacky things that life throws us into perspective. I want to talk to you, just the two of us."

So they sat and talked, and gradually it became as it was before. They were close again and Amy understood her mother's course of action taken so many years ago. A chilly mist was settling over the garden and Amy shivered, the dampness infusing her bones.

"Oh how selfish of me. You must be exhausted from your journey and starving. Why don't I show you to your room, it's made up and ready for you? Perhaps you'd like a nice warm bath while I get something for us to eat."

Amy barely heard her mother. It was as if she were in a trance. Her senses assumed a new acuity. How could she have withdrawn into herself so completely from her mother who very obviously loved and adored her and had lived so many years needing her daughter? Yes, it had been necessary for her to remove herself all those years ago but could she not have reached out and made some attempt to reconcile with her mother, at least to offer some support? No, she had not. Instead she had chosen to wallow in self-pity and close herself off from all those who had cared so much for her. How was she ever going to make amends to her mother, a true altruist who had, without hesitation, taken over the commitment of rearing her baby? In fact, would she be allowed the time to make amends?

****

The evening enveloped them in warmth and harmony as they sat by the fire sipping their Port wine. They had both enjoyed a simple yet satisfying meal set upon the table overlooking the patio and although it was summertime, the air was brisk. Typical of the south of England, there was always a chill in the evenings and early morning emanating from the sea below. Fiona was coming tomorrow. According to her mother she couldn't wait to meet her, wanting to make up for lost time. *She wants to get to know me*, Amy thought, tension gripping her like a vice. *What will she think of me? I'm hardly what one would call a proper mother. I'm a miserable failure at everything I've attempted.*

“Oh God,” she whispered a silent prayer, “please let everything be alright. Please be with me and let her understand.”

****

Amy pulled back the curtains the next morning and was greeted with a vision of such loveliness, it took her breath away. The first rays of sun cast an iridescent bloom filling the garden with a colour appearing almost contrived. Pausing, inhaling the sweet air mingled with the salt of the ocean, she almost felt guilty at succumbing to such blissful moments.

The glorious scene now lay behind her as she moved towards the bathroom to prepare herself for the day ahead and apprehension held her again in its unrelenting grasp. She wanted to run and hide. Oh yes, run and hide like she’d always done. What about poor Alex who had loved her so completely? What had she done? She’d thrown him away because she couldn’t face the implications. Simply could not take a chance on him when he had proven himself over and over and had persevered so valiantly over the years to make things up to her, trying to earn her forgiveness and now he was lost to her. She chastised herself. When was she going to face up to life, grasp it by the shoulders and get on with it? Well, life had caught up with her now and this time she had better be up to it.

She went down to breakfast filled with determination to make things right in that place, her home, that made sense of the present and held so much promise for the future.

****

Later that day, the three women sat in the sun room. The patio doors were open and a cool breeze wafted through. The sound of the waves coming to shore was drowned out periodically by the wind which was beginning to pick up. The older woman addressed her granddaughter.

"Fiona, I was wrong to send your mother and father away but they were so young, they couldn't look after you and I didn't see any other way of handling the situation. Your father insisted on paying all education for you. It was his wish that no expense would be spared on your advancement and the attainment of a profession of your choice. He has contributed monthly to your trust fund for the last twenty years."

Amy raised her eyes and looked steadfastly at her mother but said nothing. Her mother continued to address her granddaughter.

"I sent them away and you became my legal ward of court. They had no choice. They wanted the best for you but they were both too young to care for you, just kids themselves."

Fiona looked from one to the other, noting her mother's tiny worn frame echoing the years of regret. Going forward, she clasped her mother to her.

"I'm so very happy to meet you at last. We have quite a bit of catching up to do."

And that was an understatement.

Chapter 14
England Beckons

Alex had a window seat and the approach to Vancouver was more spectacular that he could ever have envisaged with its mountain ranges, valleys and lakes. Following his usual travel path, he had booked into a hotel near the airport in downtown Vancouver until he got his bearings. The city offered a huge range of good restaurants but for the first night, he elected to eat in the hotel dining room and get an early night. *Plenty of time to look around*, he thought, as his meeting with Rick, his prospective employer, was not until the following Wednesday; give him a chance to get his bearings and familiarise himself with the area.

****

Sitting across the table from Rick in the Vancouver pub a few days later, Alex was feeling very optimistic. The pair of them obviously liked each other immensely and found they had common interests.

"So, Alex, how do you like Vancouver so far?"

"I'm very impressed. It's really easy to get around and not so big that it's overwhelming. I believe I have my bearings now. I know which way the streets run and I have to say Burrard Inlet and English Bay are something else."

"Yes I really like this coast, I've been all over Canada but this is it for me."

Rick was very pleased with himself, thinking he'd hit the jackpot with Alex, a good choice and felt very much at home with him.

They chatted for a while and Rick gave a good overview of his business which he operated out of Vancouver, running tours to Vancouver Island, through Howe Sound, Sunshine Coast and to the Gulf Islands. Alex could see from the business documents Rick had brought with him for review, that the operation was extremely profitable. His job would be as Rick's backup and right-hand man, which suited him very well as he wanted to learn what he could about the tour boat business without taking the full responsibility at this stage.

Both were very excited about their first meeting and when they had finished talking business, Rick took Alex on a tour of the cruiser berthed off Vancouver. Alex had never felt envy in his life but this was a cruiser he would, well almost kill for, absolutely perfect, well maybe a little big for his purposes. Rick understood that Alex had to see other prospective employers and following up on their previous discussions, made him an offer surpassing Alex's expectations, obviously extremely keen to get him onboard. The arrangement was that they would touch base the following week when Alex had explored and reviewed his other prospects. Alex subsequently accepted Rick's offer and that was the beginning of a team effort spanning several years hence.

****

Accommodation, thought Alex as he enjoyed a leisurely breakfast, *that's the next priority*. He was feeling really good about yesterday's meeting with Rick and optimistic about the future. Leafing through the ads in the local newspaper and a couple of real estate leaflets for a rental, his eyes searched out those with a water view, the main stipulation, as always. They were all pretty expensive but he reasoned his day to day living was modest which would offset the monthly outlay. A few days later had him signed up with a one year lease. The chosen apartment catered to all his basic needs and although small, came with an outstanding view of English Bay and beyond.

****

The next few months were staggeringly busy for both men with business booming and much to learn for Alex. Rick was completely enamoured with his new crew member admiring him for his work ethic and general approach to life, much the same as his own, they were definitely on the same wavelength. Each day was a new adventure for Alex. What a truly beautiful country. His first trip to the Gulf Islands, encompassing over two hundred islands, had left him in awe. Rick focussed mainly on Gabriola, Pender and Salt Spring for his tours, each with many diverse activities and sights from the more commercial resorts to the rustic, offering havens for hikers and nature seekers. En route they were sometimes accompanied by whales and dolphins and had actually seen pods of whales following the boat.

Alex was particularly taken with Salt Spring Island, a popular centre for the arts, music and dance. The community's famed Saturday market played host to many offshore and local artists and visitors. Rick always allowed time on this particular stop over for both of them to go snorkelling and experience the exquisite array of intertidal marine life spread out before them. Snorkelling was something completely new to Alex and the Gulf

Islands offered some of the best in the world. When they weren't underwater, their cycling trips through soft, pastoral meadows and the glass of ale at the end of a long ride was always a welcome respite for both of them.

Following one of their trips and having a few days off while the boat underwent some checks, Rick arranged for a foursome. Although doubtful about the whole affair, Alex agreed to make up the numbers.

"You need to do a bit of socialising, get out of yourself for a while. You're far too reclusive," Rick had said. His girlfriend Sandy had a friend and he had been trying for months to get Alex to accompany them on a night out. Alex had steadfastly declined but Rick had caught him this time when his guard was down and being in a festive mood, he made a snap decision to meet the three of them in a downtown bar for drinks before dinner.

"Just a friendly get together." Alex had stressed, "I'm not looking for a relationship."

Having second thoughts and regretting his decision to meet up that night, Alex moved towards the bar, his gaze falling on a woman idly stirring her Bloody Mary with a stick of celery at the end of the counter. She turned her head slightly, obviously waiting for somebody. Alex stopped dead in his tracks. The resemblance to Amy was uncanny, except that she was a bigger version and her hair was dark but her mannerisms were remarkably familiar to him. She was smiling now and her eyes firmly fixed on him. Her gaze was discerningly unwavering and he felt mildly uncomfortable. Having directed the barman on his needs, he settled himself a safe distance down the bar putting enough space between them without appearing obviously rude. They each sat nursing their drinks, casting glances slyly at each other, disconcerting when their eyes met, particularly as she was obviously deriving much amusement from his embarrassment. Alex had never been practised in the art of concealment when it came to his emotions and was about to finish his drink and leave as the situation was becoming annoying, when he heard Rick's voice.

"Hi there, Alex, how are you doing friend? Let's get the party going. Angela come over here and meet Alex."

To Alex's amazement, she un-twirled her long legs from the bar stool and eased her way towards them. He had to admit she was gorgeous and as she closed in on him, he could see that her resemblance to Amy had been only fleeting. She had her own set of attributes; she didn't need to 'piggy back' on anybody else's.

The evening was fun for all four and concluded with a walk along the shore. The sunsets at English Bay were generally spectacular with the added plus that different musical groups would generally strike a few chords on warm balmy evenings. That night, it was Caribbean with all the fire and sensuality typical of the music. A couple danced barefoot in careless abandonment; their shoes flung casually to one side with the same desertion.

He knew Angela wanted to dance as she linked her arm intimately through his but he held back. It didn't escape him that Rick was watching them in a devilish way, catching his eye in what Alex recognised as a matchmaker in progress. Firmly disengaging himself from his warm companion, he called over to his friend.

"Think it's getting pretty late. Maybe we should make a move. We have a really early start in the morning."

"Yes, you're absolutely right and we still have to go over some paperwork before the first group arrive. Okay girls, party's over."

Rick was right back in the work mode.

Alex chose to ignore the disappointment on Angela's face.

"Well, it's been a great evening and a real pleasure meeting you Angela."

Making his exit quickly but graciously he headed back to his apartment.

****

"Well," said Rick in exasperation the next morning.

"You haven't said one word about her, or made one comment about the evening."

"It was a terrific evening."

"You know that's not what I meant. How did you get on with her?"

"She's a nice woman."

"Nice," Rick spluttered.

"My God, man, she's more than nice. She has a great job, she's super smart and not hard on the eyes either and she obviously has a thing for you already."

Alex just grinned.

"Yes, it was a nice evening, really terrific."

"Okay, okay got your drift. Talk about stiff upper lip; typical Brit."

"No really, it was a good evening and I was just being friendly to her, nothing more and I mean nothing more Rick. I'm not in the market."

"Okay well I hope we'll be able to make a foursome again as it was so enjoyable. It was a good break which we both needed. Sandy's been getting a bit up tight lately as we're spending so much time working."

"Yes, it was a good break and sure we'll do it again when we get time."

Rick was to hold him to that and ease Angela into Alex's world whenever he got the chance.

****

As the months passed, whenever business was a little slower, Rick would allow Sandy and Angela to accompany them by arrangement as they both needed notice to take time out from work.

This was one such trip; they were going to the Sunshine Coast, a short hop from Vancouver past English Bay and Bikini Beach. Rick explained that the beach was so named by the locals because many years previously a group of young people got together at every opportunity sporting scant swimwear, their aim being to alternate between swimming and frying their bodies in the sun. The years had lessened their number but not the enthusiasm of those remaining. These long standing diehards still gathered except their once golden, firm bodies were now coriaceous and worn, succumbing to gravity and poor versions of the sun worshippers of bygone days, albeit all were still excellent swimmers.

The journey continued via a sheltered bay, shaped by magnificent cliffs into a horseshoe and named accordingly as Horseshoe Bay and then across to the small community of Gibsons. The weather couldn't be improved upon and all four were in the best of spirits.

Alex and Rick waited for the two girls as they explored one of the little craft shops. The backcloth of Gibsons Landing was outstanding with its view of Howe Sound and the coastal mountains, mesmerising the friends as they stood.

"I just can't believe my eyes." Alex was repeating himself again.

"It's got to be one of the most sought after countries in the world. Rick if we get a chance, I wouldn't mind seeing the Art Gallery while we're here, I've heard so much about it."

“Of course, it’s just a short stroll from here and we’ll stop and have a fresh fish lunch, I know just the place.”

The excited chatter behind them cut into their conversation as Sandy and Angela came bursting out of the little store sporting a couple of packages each. The four had many such days, filled with pleasure and fun but in his quieter moments, Alex’s thoughts were never far from his home. The months became years and he buried the longing for his homeland deep within him.

****

Whenever he had any spare time, Alex usually took himself to Stanley Park. A favourite walk for him was Beaver Lake. The introduction of water lilies to the lake in the 1940s had altered the natural course of events by speeding up the return of the lake to a marsh ecosystem. While still to be enjoyed, it was apparent that the lake would be no more in the not-too-distant future.

Warm sunny days took him also to Lost Lagoon which looked as if it had been there forever but was also a product of man’s innovative architectural abilities, earning its name by disappearing when the tide turned and the water drained. Shutting off the sea water pipes solved the problem and brought about a fresh water lake which remained constant throughout the year. Alex always carried food and water with him in his knapsack, a throwback from his childhood, preferring sunny days when he could sit by the lake on his favourite bench luxuriating in the warmth of the sun and dozing, having eaten his lunch. The benches were dotted about the park and donated by people in remembrance of their loved ones who had passed.

On the rare occasion, he would see otters and even turtles present in the lake. The warm sunny days would entice the reptiles up onto the rocks to sun themselves. They actually appeared to communicate with the ducks, their heads moving in unison when the birds hopped up to share their space vocalising loudly.

His hike generally continued up to the Remembrance Gardens where he meandered through the woods by a small waterfall and pond. The gardens were created shortly after the war in memory of air force personnel who lost their lives in World War II. He stooped to clear the weeds away from the British RAF plaque pausing a few moments to honour all those brave souls who had given up their very lives in the fight for freedom. His own father came to mind, now just a vague memory of him was all that remained with Alex as he struggled to recall details of the man he had so loved and lost in such a short time span.

A man of habit, the final part of his walk invariably found him standing by a Queen Elizabeth Oak from the Royal Forest at Windsor, planted on May 12, 1937 in commemoration of the Coronation of King George V1 and Queen Elizabeth. Alex always found it incredible that the tree had been planted one year before he was even born. Displaced and struggling, it was a poor replica of the massive oak trees he had seen in England but still it stood bravely in the face of the winds which could prove quite severe blowing across from the Pacific and adjacent English Bay.

****

The phone sounded in the living room. It was Angela. Did he want to go out to see a movie or something? He didn't but thought he should make the effort as his recurring depression was resurfacing. Angela's place was on the other side of town but a pleasant walk which he welcomed. It was a fine evening and his spirits lifted as he approached her apartment building.

"Would you like a quick drink before we go?" she offered in welcome when she appeared, looking ravishing as always.

"Perhaps later, maybe we should get going, don't want to miss the show."

Once again, Alex was reluctant to be in close proximity to this stunning vision in her revealing but beautifully tailored red dress and shiny black high heeled shoes, high though they were, he still towered over her. Bob used to laugh all those years before as he measured Alex by lining him up against the door frame and putting new markers above the previous ones. It seemed that the youth grew another inch almost every time they went through this routine.

The film was a good distraction and both were in good spirits when they reached her place that evening.

"Well, are you going to have that drink now?"

She was inviting and appealing. He didn't want to spend the night alone and found himself following her through the door.

****

Alex let himself out quietly as dawn was breaking and walked slowly through the deserted streets. He had always loved walking in the early morning, so pristine, so quiet and had never lost the habit of his early days as a pauper on the London Streets. He grinned wryly wondering what Angela would have thought about that previous life of his, not much, of that he was sure.

Savouring a cup of tea later on his balcony, he watched the sunrise and reflected on the previous evening. She knew he didn't love her, purely satisfying his manly needs and sensed his irrevocable commitment to another. He saw the hurt in her eyes and hated himself for causing her pain but had no control over events. It was a two-way street, he reasoned with himself. She had pursued him relentlessly and he knew that last night had changed the entire nature of their relationship; it would never be the same again and he was right.

Over the following weeks, their meetings were strained. It was difficult to get back onto a comfortable footing and gradually by mutual agreement, they stopped seeing each other. Rick refrained from asking and ceased arranging get-togethers for the foursome. His partner and friend was distant, obviously transported elsewhere, on many occasions his eyes just fixed on the horizon staring out to sea lost on that island sitting between the North Atlantic Ocean and the North Sea.

****

Alex stood on the shore looking over the inlet at the distant peninsular; eyes half closed against the cold, lashing wind. The land mass on the horizon was reminiscent of the Isle of Wight. It was a raw day and pulling his jacket up around his neck, he saw an angry sea and an even angrier sky with clouds racing across the horizon in black fury. A 'Turner' sky always came to his mind in stormy weather; particularly Turner's 1805 Shipwreck painting. Alex likened the picture to his own experiences and the useless futility of fighting the power of an enraged sea. The paramount inferiority of man had manifested itself to him many times over the years particularly with the loss of his dear friend Jack.

Both Constable and Turner were Alex's favourite British artists. Both shared their common interest in British landscapes in the late 1700s to mid-1800s;

Constable always calm and consistent with his beautiful soft landscapes and Turner revealing the ever-evolving light and atmospheric qualities in his seascapes.

Yes, it was indeed a 'Turner' sky exhibiting that same wrath, anger and frustration Alex had unwittingly built up inside over the years. All those years without the one person who meant the most to him and without his only child—his daughter. His chest was now so compressed that the breath came in gasps as if his lungs would burst and his yearning to be home so strong it completely consumed him. The salt from his tears burned into his eyes and closing them tightly a poem came to mind hastily scribbled on a day such as this when the sickening, gnawing pain of homesickness had gripped him yet again:

Standing, watching foam capped waves roll to shore
Recalling a place so loved but dwell there no more.
In awe, mesmerised by the raging sea,
Impressive, raw, beautiful but home never to be.
Eyes now closed, resisting the brine,
Unable to stop the race back through time.
Overwhelmed and yearning to walk again
Those island beaches, my birth island`s familiar terrain. ©

He had to go home, it was long overdue. He would start making plans the next day.

The following day before breakfast he checked on flights back to England, allowing himself one month before departure to settle his affairs and give proper notice to Rick. He was going home, after all these years actually going back to England, his home, his birthplace.

Chapter 15
The Homecoming

He banged extra hard on the door, smiling at the expected response.

"Okay, okay, hold your horses; patience obviously isn't one of your virtues whoever you are."

The door was flung open and a rather abashed Bob stood there clutching his bath robe around his dripping body, having just had a perfectly good bath ruined. Wrath ebbing immediately when he saw it was Alex, his face wreathed in smiles and arms flung out in welcome.

"You're early lad; wasn't expecting you for another hour or so."

Following warm hugs all round, they made their way in yattering their heads off.

****

Sitting in Bob's little lounge later grinning at each other over their beers, each were remarking that neither had changed much over the years since they'd seen each other.

"How old are you, Bob?"

"Not sure lad, believe I'm 63. Let's see now, I was about 30 or so when I first set eyes on this scrawny little street urchin at my front door, so yes that's about right."

"Well, this street urchin has a proposition for you that hopefully will knock your socks off. Do you remember when we went south and developed a real feel for the area? The coastline is unbelievable as you know and while the sea has its moments, it's much more docile than the west coast and certainly tamer than where I've just left in Canada."

Bob was nodding sagaciously.

"I sure do, even though it was troubled times when we were down south, that day around Lymington and the coast was really something." Bob digressed, "And do you remember that mouthy bird in the New Forest pub? Every time I see any kind of a black bird I have a laugh."

Bob was leaning forward in his chair all ears.

"Go on lad, don't keep me in suspense."

"Well, I've talked about running a tour boat for years now and you knew from my letters that I was doing just that in Canada, running tours up and down the Vancouver coast."

"Yes, I wondered if you'd ever pull it off and I do remember how enthusiastic you always were about the idea. Your letters about the west coast of Canada really brought it alive to me with all its glorious islands and fabulous coastline."

Alex was getting more animated by the minute and Bob was hanging onto every word.

"Yes, Canada is truly amazing all round. It's just a pity that the weather is so extreme in most of the provinces. He shuddered remembering his tenure in eastern Canada. The west coast is perfect in that the climate is much more temperate although the rain takes a bit of getting used to but I did get a really good introduction to the boating business, thanks to Rick. By the way, he's going to be visiting us and is really excited about the prospect, so I need to get myself organised in readiness. You'll really like him.

There's no doubt about it Vancouver really firmed things up for me and had I not been so homesick, I probably would have stayed there permanently. Anyway, I decided to follow the dream and come back. I want to end up running a tour business along the south coast just taking about half a dozen people or so out at a time and I would really like you to go in with me. I have always been good with money; let's face it, after saving my own stash in the hole of a tree I know how to look after my financial affairs very seriously. I can buy the boat myself but it would be great to have you work with me in whatever capacity you feel comfortable with."

Bob was now on his feet.

"Hold the thought, Alex. I'll just refresh our glasses."

When Bob was comfortably seated again, Alex continued as he rummaged around in his faithful old back pack.

"I have pictures of the coastline, Isle of Wight, Lymington, all round the area that I'm really interested in. Take a look. I'm going back down south in a short while for a really good scout around the area. I'll research cruisers when I am there. Bob, I'm dead serious about this and please think hard about it while I'm gone."

Bob poured over the pictures, scrutinising each seriously.

"Nothing to think about, it's a great plan. I've always loved the boating life, can't tell you how much I enjoyed going out with old Harry in the early years; always had a real feel for it. It'll give me a real lift to be part of an operation like that. I could take early retirement and buy a little place there for Cathy and myself; often thought about retiring down south."

"By the way, how is Cathy? Isn't it about time you two made it permanent?"

"It's about as permanent as it ever will be. Why ruin a good thing? We've been a couple off and on since before you came on the scene. Neither of us wanted to get committed. I know she'd like a retirement option in the south; we've touched on it a couple of times. Alex, you don't know what a tonic you are lad."

"Bob, I'm hardly a lad now."

****

Years of walking about the streets of London in his earlier years and extreme physical activity at sea had served Alex well. Developing a high fitness level over the years and knowing the importance of exercise and healthy eating, he was pleased to see that there was a major movement towards organic farming and more respect for the natural countryside. He still tried to support the little grocery shops giving small business a chance to survive but more and more were being replaced by the big chain stores, which was a great pity as the personal service was also disappearing but he continued to patronise those that remained and purchased his organics wherever possible. Even Bob was getting into it enthusiastically, saying how he had almost forgotten how great steamed vegetables tasted when they were grown naturally straight from the land and not saturated in pesticides.

Alex still maintained his avid interest in the environment and general politics even when he was away from London and out of the country. He was elated that the public were very much committed to upholding the environmental sustainability of the Thames. Numerous groups were working constantly to facilitate clean-up operations; however, a new enemy was emerging; plastic, which was appearing in a mélange of varying shapes and sizes potentially threatening every ecosystem in and around the river. *Well, they've made great strides in the past*, Alex thought, *hopefully they'll be able to handle this*.

****

Rosalind and Dan had invited Alex round for a 'Good Journey South' gathering. The friends had long ago decided there would be no 'goodbyes' just good wishes every time Alex got the wander lust and this get-together was no exception. After their marriage the couple had put a deposit down on one of the basement flats in The Barbican and Alex was bursting with enthusiasm at the thought of getting a view of it first-hand. He had seen the news coverage of the official opening of the complex by the Queen in 1982 when he was away and was eager to see the new development since that time.

The estate comprised three of the highest residential towers in London, incorporating mews, terraces, sunken lake and venue for the arts and music centres, to name only a few. The entire project had become internationally recognised as one of the leading architectural achievements of the 20th century. Rosalind and Dan's home was one of the garden flats set above the sunken lake, allowing them a more scenic view when sitting and enjoying a glass of wine in the evening after their days' toils. The minute Alex walked through the door, an atmosphere of welcome engulfed him. It was obvious that this was a home filled with love.

"Dan, why don't you take Alex on a walk-around of the complex while I get dinner ready? It'll be another half hour so you have plenty of time."

Rosalind was in her element. She just loved entertaining, especially Alex as he really had an appreciation for gourmet food, well prepared with all the trimmings and was always hungry.

The tour of the complex was all that Alex could ever have imagined. The lake was exquisite, appearing so natural as if it had been there forever; an incredible example of architectural design and ingenuity. Following dinner, Dan got launched as usual, never losing his enthusiasm and support for his idle the famed black parliamentarian.

"Alex did you know that David Pitt has been elected President of British Medical Association for 1985 and '86? The man is incorrigible."

They were enjoying a glass of port and Alex raised his glass.

"To my friends, a heartfelt thanks for a culinary delight and to say how privileged I feel to have friends such as you. This is a lovely home exuding goodwill and I can see your cup 'runneth over' with happiness. My very best to you now and always my friends and when I'm settled down south you'll come and grace my table and enjoy the benefits of the south coast."

Alex was pontificating to the extreme and all three howled with laughter at the sheer cheek of the man.

"I just couldn't help it," Alex said expansively, finally coming up for air. "I was feeling affluent, we are so very fortunate, we have so much and have come from so little, material wise that is."

"That would be super. We'd love to come." Dan was flushed with well-being and not in small part to the port which he made himself. This latest batch was particularly pungent and aged over a year.

"Talking of visiting, what's going to happen to this place of yours on the west coast? That little community gave us the best welcome and honeymoon we could ever have had when we stayed there. The people were so kind and welcoming and your place is out of this world. Are you going to hang on to it?"

"Of course I am. I'll take time out periodically to go down. Bob is completely enamoured with it and has been down a few times already with Cathy. I'll keep it as long as I am able to get down there. It's only a few hours away."

****

As always, his time with his best friend and now his beautiful wife also, was quality time. As he strode down the road, he was thinking once again just how exceptionally lucky he was to have such friends. They were the best, couldn't have wished for better.

Tomorrow he was getting together with Sid and Elsie. They were going to give him a good send off and Bob too was looking forward to it. Elsie's cooking and Sid's baking were an awesome combination.

"Better prepare yourself for another emotional parting Alex, when old Elsie gets going, there's no stopping her. We'd better make a quick exit before she really gives in to it."

Bob could never get into too much 'emotional crap' as he called it. He simply couldn't handle it. He did notice; however, that Alex managed to refrain from asking how Amy was doing. Amy had left some time ago and Bob was not privy to her whereabouts. He had asked Sylvia numerous times if she had heard from her daughter but she had not and they had not been in touch with each other for quite a while.

Amy had been deteriorating for some time and he wasn't surprised when she simply gave notice to Sid and left, giving no forwarding address. She was lost now; had been for years, simply going through the motions of life. It was as if she had completely shut down. He didn't want the subject broached as there was nothing to be done and the last thing he wanted to do at this late stage in the game was to get into it with Alex. The whole issue saddened him whenever he thought of the love those two had shared, young though they had been and now it seemed that the very loving had destroyed both of them.

****

Alex's hotel room overlooked the ocean. The day had been another exhausting one, familiarising himself with the area and he was tired. Nursing his drink he lost himself in the skies rich in colour of every hue. The setting sun heralded the night with glorious rays fanning out in every direction, casting red shadows on the sway; a red ball of fire on its downhill slide behind the horizon and into the sea it seemed.

Turning his thoughts to the project at hand, he figured with his background knowledge he shouldn't have too much trouble establishing himself in a little business. Quite apart from his regular marine updates, he had acquired business accreditation over the recent years and felt himself well placed and in a strong position to operate a business of his own. Yes his visit had thus far been successful. He'd researched possible cruisers and moorage locations and figured he wouldn't have too many problems other than the initial 'start-up' headaches. Satisfaction filled his being. Now business preliminaries were sorted out, he would concentrate on personal matters.

He was going to find Amy and Fiona and he would start with Amy's mother. Since his final financial contribution for Fiona's education, he had not been in touch with Sylvia and wondered how she would receive him, assuming she still lived in the same house. He would look her up tomorrow but right now he needed a good bath, food and rest.

****

She had her back to him, bent over tending her roses. Her wide brimmed straw hat decorated with flowers shrouded her face as her fingers worked deftly with the secateurs.

My God, she's worn well, he thought, anxiously wondering what sort of a reception she would give him. The formal handing over of their baby to her was indelible in his mind; he hoped she'd receive him without animosity after all these years; he only wanted to find her daughter, Amy.

Aware of his step on the path, she straightened and turned. Their eyes met and with an intake of breath, he could see he was gazing into the sweet face of the woman he had loved practically all his life.

"Amy, my dearest Amy."

She was unmoving as her eyes locked with his.

"Hello Alex, how are you? It's been a long time."

The air was electric, charged with emotion.

"Come inside, it's so hot. I'll get you some homemade lemonade."

Extending her hand, she hooked her arm in his and they walked slowly to the house. It was as natural as if they had never been apart.

As they approached the door, a young dog came bounding towards them.

"Alex, meet Kali, Kali, meet Alex."

He stayed that night and somehow never got around to leaving.

Chapter 16
Business and Pleasure

Alex and Amy took a walk by the waterfront and part of the way along the great coastal walk. They had taken their lunch with them and stopped to admire the stunning view of the Needles and the Isle of Wight. As they sat, Amy spoke of the love she had for their caring, compassionate daughter and how Fiona had given so selflessly to her when her mother had died, sparing no effort in trying to keep her mind off the sad occasion of Sylvia's passing, always making herself available, always organising little day trips when the loss of her grandmother must have weighed so heavily on her own shoulders. The three had grown very close over the years, enjoying many special times together. What a blessing they'd all found each other in time.

"And what a blessing you didn't give up on me, Alex," she added. "What an incredible journey our lives have taken with such an enduring love. I'm so very grateful to have inherited this beautiful house that we can share and make a real home together for the rest of our lives."

Arm in arm, shoulder to shoulder, both paused to reflect on their lives and the everlasting love they'd shared. The warmth of the sun seeped into their bones and saturated them with contentment. Amy finally broke the silence.

"On a different note, I suppose we'd better draw this sweet interlude to a close. The boats will be in soon and we have to pick up the fresh fish for dinner. Bob and Cathy will be arriving at about six o'clock and we have quite a bit of ground to cover before then. I want to take a last look at their room and make sure they have everything they need, particularly as they may be staying with us for some time while they are house hunting."

Alex agreed, reluctantly getting up and pulling her onto her feet.

"What better way to end a perfect day than to spend an evening with our best friends. We got lucky Amy; oh boy did we ever get lucky."

****

"Alex, they're here. Bob and Cathy have arrived. I can hear them outside the door."

Drying her hands, she called him from the kitchen patio, pausing to watch him feverishly tearing off his gloves. *He's turned into quite a gardener and expert in organic growing. Imagine planting marigolds between the rows of vegetables because they are insect repellent. Goodness knows where he picked that up from but it certainly works and there certainly isn't the same need for pesticides. Yes, he really is a man of many talents,* she was thinking. Their table was constantly graced with an assortment of delectable vegetables and fruits and since installing his greenhouse, Alex had been in his element. A longer growing period and her freezer were turning them into regular homesteaders.

She stayed to watch him for a moment longer as he staggered up the path with a basket laden with vegetables and Kali getting under his feet at every opportunity directing operations. *What an incredible man, what stamina with all the trials in his life, still so handsome sporting a full head of silver hair with undertones of the original blond.* Still longer, she lingered just watching him. *No man could ever match up to him.* Finally reaching the kitchen, he set his basket down on the counter and she wrapped her arms around him in tender embrace.

"What's all this about?" He was smiling at her, his crooked smile peeling the years away from his rugged features.

They heard Bob and Cathy chortling away before she could reply. The two were in the hallway by this time, obviously enjoying one of Bob's lurid jokes. Their moment was gone, as all moments must.

"We'd better break this up my lady," and winking down at her, "Won't look good if the host and hostess are upstairs or something."

Bedlam ensued; the best kind of bedlam as when one's dearest friends are coming to visit.

Amy came rushing down the hall drying her hands again with Alex in hot pursuit. Bob and Cathy managed to get stuck in the corner of the hall with the suitcases, Kali succeeded in getting under everybody's feet again; hugs all around and laughter permeated the walls.

Later when they were are all sitting down, Bob held the floor as usual.

"Just as well we're all down here for a fresh start, I was going to have to do major renovations converting to North Sea gas or oil now that Margaret Thatcher has shut down all the mines. Anyway, all the easy coal has already been taken and what with the miners' impractical demands, mining just isn't a viable proposition any longer. So taken all round, the move has worked out really well for me. I prefer gas anyway."

"Yes, so do I," Cathy piped up, "guess who will be going house hunting tomorrow? Isn't it exciting? Perhaps you'd like to come with us Amy."

Nodding, Amy directed her gaze to Alex.

"Alex have you told them about your boating friend's place?"

"I was about to princess but I can't get a word in edgewise."

They all had a laugh and Amy rushed to get more refreshments from the kitchen followed closely by Alex. He swept her off her feet.

"You look particularly delectable today, my princess."

"As do you my prince. Now you'd better get back in there to our guests and tell them about your friend's house. Do you think you can take some of this food in for me please?"

Alex continued where he had left off and they were all back in the lounge munching on their goodies.

"As I was saying, Rudy and Zoe have this really great place just up from the water but it's only good for two and now that she's expecting they have to sell. It's a tiny little cottage not far from here with a great view of the water as well; would be perfect for you two. Do you think you might like to take a look at it?"

The following day saw Bob with an agreement in place. Alex was secretly impressed because while he knew the price of the cottage was fair, it was still substantial because of the location. Old Bob's business with a bit of this and a bit of that certainly brought in the bread by the looks of it and big dividends to boot. He gave Bob a knowing wink when his friend showed him the contract.

"Just reciprocating, Bob. Remember how you winked when I deposited my first sum of money in the bank from my cache in the tree. Have to say old friend, I'm impressed."

“As I was and am with you, really impressed that you can come up with the kind of cash that you’ve been talking about for starting up a tour boat business. The moorage costs alone in this area are enough to scupper anybody. You’ve never looked back that’s for sure. Good on you lad.”

“Well I know it’s expensive but look what you get, easy access in and out at any tide and only a short hop to open water.”

The two friends were really enthusiastic about starting the tour business. Alex hadn’t realised that Bob was out on many boating trips with Harry over the years and more than qualified when it came to running a vessel, having remained certified and abreast of the boating industry trends and regulations over the years. He was also unaware of just how serious Bob had been about retiring to a seafaring community down south. The correlation of their plans was a revelation to both, a real bonus to be travelling the same course.

They spent the rest of the day on the boat with Alex, giving Bob a full tour. Even though the vessel was Amy’s favourite of all the ones they had seen; he wanted Bob to have a preview before the final purchase and had put a hold on it, pending the completion of the sale.

It was a two engine powerful cruiser which could accommodate eight comfortably with a couple of bathrooms and en-suite off the master cabin, very spacious with a large viewing lounge and saloon, an aft deck and even a roomy fly deck for those with stronger stomachs. Bob was really impressed. Alex grinned all over his face.

“What do you think about this high pressure diving compressor for deep-sea diving? I thought it would make a great optional extra if we ever took out some diving enthusiasts.”

Bob slapped Alex on the back and grabbed his hand and began shaking it vigorously.

"Yep, no argument there, looks like you've thought of everything and this vessel would certainly handle some long distance cruising if required. I'm really taken with the clear visibility from both helm positions. I think this is a really good choice, you certainly know how to pick 'em.

On a more serious note, Alex, you've waited a lot of years for this and I must confess, so have I. I thought we might never get the opportunity to work together on a venture such as this and I feel really good about the whole thing. Just want you to know I'm thrilled to bits and so is Cathy. Her mouth has been going non-stop she's so excited about this new phase in our lives."

"I agree, absolutely. It's a really special time for all of us."

*****

Alex received an excellent price break from the vendor, nevertheless still ended up spending a prodigious amount of money but he didn't care and filled with exuberance, rushed home to relay the day's events to Amy.

He found her in the bedroom sitting on the edge of the bed, her little treasure box on her lap. He recognised the little box. The first time he set eyes on it was when he rescued her from the street. She had taken it out of her knapsack all those years ago when he first met her. He remembered again his little tin box which he too had kept all these years. It had held his most precious possessions when, as an orphaned boy, he was forced to take to the streets to avoid being sent to an orphanage or worse exported as a pauper to one of the commonwealth countries.

She was reading something.

"Alex, sit down for a minute. I want you to read dear Frank's note which he wrote to me just before he passed. Look at this little rhyme, I didn't show it to anyone at the time as you know there was so much going on for all of us. What a dear sweet man he was. I think about him often."

She patted the bed beside her and the two sat closely while Alex read the words of an old man who had loved him and the teen girl as if they were his own.

****

The following days were a frenzy of madness. Cathy and Amy were engrossed in setting up Bob and Cathy's new house. Alex and Bob were wholly absorbed in plotting routes and putting their business in place. They both agreed that their tour radius initially would be around the Isle of Wight and later provide customised tours allowing stops en route at selected towns, each with a charm of their own and offering individual attractions. Their main focus would be on towns such as Cowes, the International Sailing Centre and host of world class regattas, Newport with its main shopping centre and the Victorian town Ryde with its miles of sandy beaches and the oldest pier in the world. The island offered so much diversity.

They would be arranging for brochures to be printed up soon and getting their accountant/bookkeeper on board. The business would be run initially from Alex's office in the house and their plan was to eventually have a formal office a little later down the road. When the accountant issue had come up, Bob had immediately put

Alex in touch with Mani, his own accountant. Alex was more than a little pessimistic about the business arrangement.

"Now Bob, I'm sure that Mani is one of the best but I have some concerns."

"Yeah, yeah," Bob was interrupting again.

"And I'm pretty sure what they are. Listen Alex, I'm strictly legit now. No more subversive stuff, strictly kosher. I'm not an idiot. I know we're reaching out to the upper echelon on this tour business; the last thing I'm going to do is jeopardise it. Mani knows the score. There will be no, absolutely no fiddling with the books, strictly above board we definitely don't want to get caught with our pants down. Don't worry lad, I'll not let you down."

The freckled nosed kid was grinning broadly right back at him.

"It's a funny thing Bob, those words seem familiar. Wasn't it some snotty nosed street urchin that said the same to you some thirty odd years ago?"

True to form their guffaws almost brought the roof down.

Chapter 17
Peace

"Wake up sleepy head."

Amy wore a pair of faded, torn pale-blue jeans with a rose coloured shirt, exactly the same as all those years ago when he first saw her except she was no longer a street waif, now she was a beautiful mature woman, freshly scrubbed from the shower, glowing and carrying his breakfast tray to him.

"Remember our first meal, how you laid the table for me in the old theatre with all the trimmings?"

Alex was struggling with a wealth of pillows in an effort to sit up.

"Oh I remember alright and how you ribbed me about being your king taking you back to my castle."

She was laughing and he laughed with her, joyous, boundless laughter.

****

The next day was a flurry of activity with everything being scrubbed and cleaned including poor Kali and baking galore wafting delightful odours from the kitchen. Alex; however, was having a hard time. He sat nervously in the little sun room, book unread lying in his lap; his mind back in the past.

They had been barely 16 years old when their daughter was born. So many years of their lives had passed, so deeply their transgression had been carried on their backs through each one, weighing on both so heavily. His dear Amy's life's project had been to inflict more abuse on her poor body and mind and his only recourse work, work and more work until he almost dropped, taking life threatening risks just for the hell of it. He had loved her more than life itself.

Head in hands, he felt the onset of despair but his spirit rallied. What about all the wonderful people he had met over the years? What about the travel and most of all what about the final, wonderful bonding with his soulmate and the beautiful human being they had both created?

Fiona was coming and would be here soon. Finally he was going to meet his daughter, his one and only sight of her had been as a newborn when he had held her in his arms so briefly. Through the years, that moment and her warm baby freshness had stayed with him to haunt him. He was more nervous now than when he skippered his first boat. What would she think of him? Would she consider him a successful father? He didn't think he could stand another minute of waiting to find out. Getting to his feet, allowing the book to fall to the floor, he started pacing. He could see the ocean as he slipped through the French doors onto the little patio. *How calm and tranquil the water was today, unlike me*, he thought, his mind in turmoil.

Hearing voices, he turned. The sight before him took his breath away. Amy, exquisite in her floral print dress, so typically English. Anybody looking at her would recognise her British heritage, even without her opening her mouth. A gorgeous, almost identical younger version of her moved confidently across the room smiling warmly. He didn't know whether to shake her hand or what? Quite unabashed, she threw her arms around his neck and the two clung to each other for a few moments, both faces awash with tears. Amy looked on, grinning like a Cheshire cat then all three were talking at once. After all, they had to catch up on the last 30 odd years. Fiona was staying for a few days and they had a full agenda, particularly as she was anxious to see their boat moored at Lymington.

"Fiona, perhaps you would like to go out on her tomorrow. I'll invite Bob and Cathy, they're dying to meet you. Would that be okay with you? We could all take a picnic and have a run up the coast. In fact we could actually go over to the Isle of Wight and stay a night. What do you think of that?"

"Oh how fabulous, Dad, yes I'd love that and it's absolutely terrific that I get to meet your friends. What a super surprise."

Alex started at the word 'dad'. *My God, how strange, I'm only a few years older than my own daughter... mind boggling.*

The next day saw the group piling down the steps to the harbour staggering under the weight of their picnic and overnight supplies, as they had unanimously agreed on a night stop off the Island.

Fiona didn't have to wonder which boat was her dad's. There it was with huge black script lettering 'Amy's Choice'. Alex had insisted that Amy pick out the one she really wanted and she had no hesitation in picking this triple decker with spacious sleeping arrangements and plenty of room on the main deck and lounge for tourists.

"All aboard then."

Alex was inordinately proud of his cruiser and delighted that Fiona, who was squealing enthusiastically, took to it immediately, as he helped her up the gang plank. Cathy eased her brightly clad, rubenesque figure up the incline with Bob's hand firmly on her elbow, the pair of them giggling as always like a couple of school kids looking as if they'd just won first prize and Amy bringing up the rear, positively galloping up after them with Kali, now the seafaring hound of the south coast.

Their trip took them around the east coast of the island past Ventnor, Shanklin, Sandown and finishing at Ryde where they enjoyed ambling through the Victorian architecture, finally quenching their thirst with a lager and lime on the patio of a gracious old pub which accommodated dogs, the owners welcoming them with a large bowl of water for Kali on the patio. It was a happy group that revelled in the comfort of 'Amy's Choice' that evening. All equipment had checked out on the vessel and it had been an excellent trial run in readiness for business. Bob and Alex breathed a sigh of relief as they had both been keeping their fingers and toes crossed that nothing would go wrong.

****

The new business took off like a house on fire and they were booked steadily throughout the major part of the year. Customised tours had been incorporated, taking in the many functions and regattas and even dinosaur and fossil hunting expeditions that the Isle of Wight offered.

Somehow or other Alex and Bob managed to search out and sign the lease of their new business premises. The retrofit and set up of their new office space to receive and provide information to the general public was a major achievement considering how busy they were with the tours. The new coloured signage was eye catching and very professional and as the graphics company had a business branch dealing with professional business cards, stationary, etc. Alex was able to score a 'wicked' deal by having all the company's paper needs handled under contract.

Cathy now ran the front office assisted by Zoe who was her backup. Zoe was fortunate to have her mother around to help out with her young son and she loved working in the office to keep herself 'centred' as she called it. Having always been employed in various offices, she was very accomplished; a successful arrangement for all concerned.

Rudy also became a valuable contributor to the business assisting Alex and Bob. As a licensed yachtsman with many years' seafaring experience, he was a major asset to the business and both Alex and Bob considered themselves extremely fortunate to have been able to entice him into the company. They were all compatible with each other and made a great group both businesswise and on a social basis, enjoying many grand get-togethers alternating around each of their homes.

****

The days, months, years all rolled into one. Poor old Kali had passed on years before to be superseded by her relative of two generations hence. Almost identical in looks but finely made, hence her name 'Willow', a gentle creature, the same as Kali had always been.

****

That night sitting next to each other gazing into the flames of the fire in the little parlour, they were close, closer than they had ever been before, almost as if they were one; each locked in thought. They had been enjoying some wine; their empty glasses caught the fire light casting an iridescent glow. The old dog's feet twitched as she slept, in her own world of good smells and thousands of squirrels and rabbits.

Alex noted for the first time how worn and frail his sweet Amy was. Her earlier years of hardship and abuse of her body were definitely telling on her. He gently moved a lock of hair from her eyes and tenderly put his arm around her shoulders.

"Amy, you have never forgiven yourself or me for our indiscretion. Please put it aside, I implore you. It was so long ago, so very long ago."

She returned his affection suddenly putting her arms around him and holding him tight and for the first time she addressed the turmoil each had lived with for so long.

"Alex, I want you to know I have always loved you ever since I first set eyes on you. You were the only one for me. I have always wanted you to hold me, love me but never to make love to me ever again and I'm sorry, so very sorry. The guilt of our irresponsibility weighed so heavily on me that something froze inside me and died. So long ago, so much time wasted, so much regret. Please forgive me. I've wasted our lives and precious time we could have spent together."

"Don't Amy, please don't lash yourself like this. It's done and over. We're blessed, we've had these wonderful years together and have a beautiful daughter who loves us in spite of all and although we've been apart, we have always been together in spirit. Our love has always been deep and everlasting."

Tears were trickling down his cheeks dropping onto her upturned face. His heart clenched, she was not strong; he knew that. Every day she lost a little more energy.

"Amy, it's always been only you for me, there's been no other."

Her eyelids now closed were akin to tiny pink shells bordered by lashes fanning out like delicate daisy petals on pale cheeks. He sat for a while at peace just for being with her, totally enthralled, his gaze never leaving her face.

Opening her eyes, suddenly she met his scrutiny head on.

"Alex, of course I forgive you and I've finally forgiven myself. At last, I can rest easy and you're here with me and that's all that matters."

She slept then and very carefully so as not to waken her he lifted her, carried her to her little bedroom at the end of the hall and laid her on the soft down floral eiderdown. How ashen she was but how infinitely beautiful as she lay amongst the flowers she loved so much displayed all over her bedding. He sat for a long time by her side cherishing every precious moment.

Finally in his own bed, his sleep was fitful and he repeatedly checked on Amy, always pausing for a few minutes to marvel again at her exquisite little form. She looked like an angel, so tranquil, as she reposed in sleep. How lucky they'd been to have had these years together in peace and happiness.

The next morning he moved slowly into the day. He thought he'd go downstairs and make a special breakfast for himself and Amy.

There she was on the kitchen floor. He stood transfixed, twelve years old again and engulfed in that deadly freezing cold so familiar to him, remembering another time when these same feelings had enveloped him totally and completely. Stooping and cradling her head in his lap, he remained for a long time and prayed as he had for his mother.

Full circle, I've gone full circle, he thought. Gently laying her head down, he stood heartbroken, gazing down at her the love of his life. Grief absorbed his whole being but he felt a strange calmness. He was at peace with himself as she was.

The next few days were a haze of people, arrangements and the cremation which Amy had wanted. Fiona was wonderful and at his side throughout. Amy had left the house to him. She knew he loved it as much as she did; it would be in good hands and life would remain much the same for old Willow.

Fiona was coming tomorrow. She was bringing the new man in her life; it seemed that he might be the one; they obviously had deep feelings for each other. A smile came to his lips, he remembered when he had first brought Amy to meet dear old Frank a life-time ago and yet it seemed like yesterday.

He sat listening to the rain pattering on the window, sounding like the delicate chinking of glasses and imagined them again toasting each other by the firelight as they had done so often these past years. He could hear her laughter as they both looked down at the old dog, always in between them relishing every moment. Amy never tired of saying, "Take a look at that old dog gazing up at us; just look at the love in her eyes."

Dear Amy, his precious Amy gone, body taken from him but she was with him still, her spirit lingering in this house, their home. He raised his glass to his lips.

"To you, my sweet love."

And the old dog looked up at him with love in her eyes.